THE MAN WHO LOVED STEPHEN KING

Faustin Charles

Published by BookPublishingWorld

Copyright©FaustinCharles 2019

Cover design by Kysha Charles

ISBN 978-1-5262-0714-2

BookPublishing World is an imprint of Dolman Scott Ltd
www.dolmanscott.co.uk

For Dalia, Kysha, Chewan,
Michael and Joseph who
love stories and waited
a long time for this homage

BY THE SAME AUTHOR

NOVELS:
SIGNPOSTS OF THE JUMBIE
THE BLACK MAGIC MAN OF BRIXTON
JUMBIE STOLE THE INNOCENCE
A CARIBBEAN VAMPIRE IN LONDON

STORIES:
TALES FROM THE WEST INDIES
UNCLE CHARLIE`S CRICK CRACK TALES

POETRY:
THE EXPATRIATE
CRAB TRACK
DAYS AND NIGHTS IN THE MAGIC FOREST
CHILDREN OF THE MORNING
SEA POEM

PLAYS:
HEROES OF EMANCIPATION

FOR CHILDREN:
THE SELFISH CROCODILE
THE SELFISH CROCODILE NURSERY RHYME BOOK
ED. A CARIBBEAN COUNTING BOOK
ED. KISKADEE QUEEN
ED. UNDER THE STORYTELLER`S SPELL
WILKIE AND THE BAKOO
ANANCY MAN(Operetta)
GREEDY SNAKE
TEACHER ALLIGATOR
ONCE UPON AN ANIMAL

Only in men`s imagination does every truth find an effective and undeniable existence.....**Joseph Conrad**

If you can tell stories, create characters, devise incidents, and have sincerity and passion, it doesn`t matter a damn how you write.....**Somerset Maugham**

Author`s note

This novel is a homage to Stephen King who has opened up areas of creative fiction unimagined by most creative writers of the twentieth-century. And who has re-claimed the art of storytelling as the true vehicle for the dissemination of fiction.

F.C.

1

Old man Prince was seen every day about six a.m. in the morning taking a walk, dressed in a new suit for every day of the week. Whatever the weather, he never missed a day. He lived alone in a big grey brick house on a little hill near a forest. Prince preferred the sunlight. He loved it when the rays penetrated his face and body and made him feel young and rejuvenated. Prince said that all his family: his children and grandchildren had grown-up, married and moved away, some of them abroad, and they seldom kept in touch with him. No one knew his age, some guessed he was in his eighties, others that he was beyond that, and there were others who thought that he was a hundred or over. His clothes fitted him impeccably, shoes always shone, ties matched his well-tailored suits.

The Princes were a well-known prominent family who had made a lot of money from overseas trade and oil. As a child Sidney Prince loved to read, all his interest was in reading.

He loved taking part in school plays and concerts, most of all, he loved story-books, stories about magic and wonder. Whenever he read, a glow appeared on his face, his senses became sharper and he seemed to enter the story he was reading. He was completely taken over by the events in the tale. Sometimes his parents snapped him out of it, but as soon as that happened he passed out. His worried parents took him to specialists but they found nothing wrong with him.

Sidney had a sister, his junior, her name was Carron. His mother read to him when he was a small child, even when he was a baby and all through his boyhood. Sidney was something of a genius: he began reading at the age of two; no one taught him to do so, and he was a sensation at school. He read adult books as a child as well.

It was said that Sidney Prince was reading when he was in his mother`s womb. When he was born, he didn`t come into the world crying but reciting, ONCE UPON A TIME, his baby-eyes bulged and glowed like the brightest stars.

Sidney was a voracious reader, he read books many adults found difficult. His deepest interest was in the supernatural and horror fiction as he grew older. As a child he was never scared of the horror in the stories, he revelled in them. He was never interested in toys and games. His room was had shelves stacked with his favourite books. He had two best friends who lived lower down the little hill and who attended the same private school. There was Ricky or Richard, a bright boy who loved games, especially computer-games, and Timothy, a shy, quiet boy who loved computers most of all. Ricky and Timothy couldn`t understand Sidney; they didn`t dislike reading nor stories but thought reading, and the intense reading of Sidney was only for serious school study, of course, they loved comic-books.

In fact, all the children at Sidney`s school thought he was strange and boring. And Sidney narrated the stories which he knew by heart; the way he did this was as if he was experiencing the events in the stories, he thought it was the greatest fun and thrill transmitting the tales to listeners. He was always in the school`s library at break-times instead of going out to play, and he was always at the public library when he wasn`t at school.

"I`m very good friend of Jack!" he said one day coming out of the school`s library. "The giant can`t catch us!"

A group of children looked at him strangely ran off.

"Hurry! Hurry! Down the Beanstalk tree!" he called out. "We must get away! Mother!

Mother! Quick! The axe! Cut it! Cut it! That`s it!" And he threw his arms in the air jubilantly.

The teachers found Sidney extremely fascinating, bright and eager to learn. From an early age, Sidney began to think what it would be like to get into a story and become part of it without changing anything. That was the magic he aspired to, to l ive in a tale. Sometimes sleeping and waking, he heard a storyteller`s voice calling, calling him. At school and at home, stories rang in his head: JACK AND THE BEANSTALK, HANSEL AND GRETEL, LITTLE RED RIDING HOOD, DRACULA, THE LAIR OF THE WHITE WORM, SHE, and others he knew by heart.

Sidney`s father was tall, six feet and slender; his mother was a small woman just over five feet and very pretty with brown hair and blue eyes. Sidney`s sister was a frail girl withgrey eyes and blond hair, like her father`s. Sidney on the other hand inherited his father`s built and his mother`s brown hair.

"Where have you been?" Carron asked as she saw her brother in an excited state coming in from outside. "Mum was worried, she thought you were in your room?"

"I`ve been playing with Ricky," Sidney said, his face showing sweat; he stood in the large hallway for a while; it was late afternoon on a sunny Saturday in mid-April, then he went to his room, sat on the bed and looked at the books in his room and sighed deeply. A bright ray of sunlight came through his half-opened window and spotlighted his face now red, it seemed to move around the room, spotlighting the books. And faraway, he heard voices, slowly it occurred to him the voices were coming from the spotlighted books. He heard: "Bring me my hen that lays golden eggs!" Bring me my golden harp!" "I`ll grind his bones to make my bread!" And a voice whispered in his ear: "Come, Sidney. When are we going to see you?" The sunray on his face was brighter.

Another time he was reading, "Ali Baba and the Forty thieves", when he heard the galloping of horses` hoofs and a voice commanding: "Open Sesame!" Then after a while, "Close Sesame!" Then hoofs galloping again. He was sweating all over and his head ached slightly. Oh, I want to live in stories, become a character in them, he thought, wished and prayed. And the voice whispered, "Read, read more!"

"Sid! Sid! Are you there?" another voice was calling him, he opened the door, it was his sister. He came out of his room in a dreamy daze. "What is it now?" he asked her dreamily.

"Ricky wanted you," Carron replied, her eyes searching his face.

The Princes house was a three-storeyed building with extensive lawn trees and flower-gardens of roses and other flowers all around the detached house. The Princes owned the house which bordered Ricky`s family home. The Princes` house was walled around with large back and front lawns. Sidney`s and Carron`s rooms and a bathroom were on the third floor; their parents` bedroom and bathroom were on the second floor. The other rooms were for visiting family or guests. Kitchen, dinning-room, sittingroom were on the first floor, French-windows led out into the back lawn and garden. the house was painted light grey and white.

The house was situated on the outskirts of the city; the front of the house faced a quiet tree-lined cul-de-sac with similar dwellings.

As he came outside, the sun fell on his face with the biggest smile. Ricky was also smiling, they went to the back garden of Sidney`s house. Sidney wondered about telling Ricky and Timothy his secret. It was Sunday morning before noon. Ricky loved climbing trees, although he was told not to do so by his parents and teachers, because some months ago he fell and badly hurt his back; sometimes he ignored the warnings, he began to climb a small lime tree but was interrupted by Carron who came out to the back.

"You were told not to!" she called to him sternly.

Ricky changed his mind about climbing, and said, "Let`s play football!"

Sidney nodded, "Yes, all right," somewhat disinterested.

"May I play too," asked Carron, smiling and coming between the boys

"Yes, you, all right. I can`t see why not," Ricky giggled.

From the side of the house, Ricky picked up a blue-and-white football, kicked it to Sidney who kicked it to his sister who surprisingly kicked it over the small lime tree.

"Wow! Great kick!" Ricky shouted.

"You mean for a girl," Carron put in, then smiled.

The day was warm, not hot.

Sidney went to get the ball, but he seemed to be floating in the air over the lime tree.

"What! How! It`s" Ricky stuttered, dumbfounded.

Carron got somewhat cross-eyed, "Mum! Dad!" she called to the house. Her Dad was out and her mother was on the telephone in the sittingroom.

Sidney came down slowly in slow motion, clinging to the ball against his chest

"When did you learn to do that Kung Fu jump?" Ricky came to him in a dazed, puzzled look; he couldn`t believe what he just saw.

"Oh, I`ve been practising jumping up and down on my bed like a trampoline," Sidney lied. He was overcome with admiration.

Carron didn`t know what to make of it. Boys are always up to some prank, she thought. Still, it was amazing and she was proud of her brother. She certainly didn`t want to doubt and embarrass her brother in front of his best friend and neighbour. But she wondered and wondered.

"And I`ve also been practising basket-ball jumps," Sidney went on lying.

The fact was, as Sidney read the story-books of magic and wonder he was experiencing magical powers. He wanted desperately to tell his family and friends but thought that they would all think he was a freak or ill or going mad.

A gentle breeze rustled the surrounding trees, played with the flowers and carried a sweet fragrance all around the scene.

All Sidney`s school-work was brilliant. The more he read, the better he progressed. The teachers marvelled at his achievements. His senses became sharper and more focused and he developed a remarkable memory. His biggest worry was whether to share his new found powers with anyone. His mental capacities developed more than his physical capacities. Maybe it was because he didn`t like sports and games: he liked watching sports and games on television, that was all . He played with his friends at home and school sometimes but he never lost himself in any physical game.

At nights when children were supposed to be fast asleep in their beds, Sidney would be reading about genies, giants,witches, goblins, dwarfs, magic carpets, sorcerers, animals changing into people and people changing into animals and fairies enchanting children.

It was on a dark gloomy early winter night, the sky was starless and sulky, suggesting rain and even a storm that

Sidney met a lovable, talkative old man hobbling along the pavement about two blocks from his home. The old man dragged his feet, he could hardly lift them. As they came close to each other, the old man smiled a wrinkled, worn smile and said, "Goodnight, young man!"

"Goodnight,sir," Sidney answered and wasn`t afraid.

"It looks as if it`s going to rain," the old man looked up at the sky. He was dressed in blue suit, white shirt, striped tie and black shoes. "I should `ve brought my umbrella. But then again, never mind, rain never hurt anyone."

Sidney`s eyes searched the old man`s worn-out and tired face, and with his heightened sense of sight – his vision was like xray vision – the old man`s face seemed ancient, prehistoric, lined like an old landscape. The old man`s complexion was very pale and his eyes had a dead, faraway look in them.

Sidney imagined that the old man`s body must be nothing more than skin and bones.

The old man seemed to guess Sidney`s curiosity, and said, "Yes, I`m a very, very old man. But I still love to take my walks at anytime of the day or night. A lot of fresh air is good at whatever age you are. And what are you doing out at this time of night?"

Sidney was a little puzzled; what should he answer. Should he tell the old man about his reading-powers? That sometimes he hears voices calling him, and sometimes he goes out to find out who was calling and where they were, whether night or day, "I`m afraid, I`ve somehow lost my way," Sidney ventured.

And again the old man seemed to read Sidney`s thoughts. "Never mind that, my son.

We`re all going for a walk to get some fresh air.

Suddenly the sky brightened and a moon appeared, lighting up the old man`s face.

"Oh, we`re in luck," the old man`s face now took on a jubilant smile. "It`s not going to rain. It might turn out to be a nice night after all. I know about the voices you`ve been hearing in your reading powers. Be very careful. And tell no one. As you get older, you`d see wonders beyond the imagination of any reader. The science-fiction stories of H.G Wells are there to give you more strength."

Sidney began to feel wonderful, his spirits were lifted into the smile of the now brighter moon.

"My son, a book is a world," the old man continued somewhat wearily. "I`ve travelled through worlds of many storytellers, and they have guided me through a very long and enchanted life. I`m ageless. I`m a character of a million faces. I`m the reality of dreams. And, while it is great for a writer to receive prizes and honours The most important thing for any writer of books is, a vast readership. Without readers, a writer isn`t a writer" As the old man spoke his voice shook.

The moon was smiling brighter than ever now like an over-full moon, and the surrounding trees and hedgerows were still. Slowly, the old man began to disappear and as he did so, his broken-up voice called, "Read! Read! Re..a...d... Rea....d! And ......and be careful what you read!" Then the old man was gone. But a faraway voice called, "Perhaps we shall meet again!"

Sidney came out of the meeting with the old man like from a dream, he was fast asleep in his room. The dream seemed so real.

"Sid! Sid!" his mother knocked on his door. "It`s time to get up for school! He Jumped out of bed, feeling refreshed.

Sidney was ten years old. Although he read adult books, he was growing into adulthood reading children`s stories. He flew like Peter Pan when no one was looking. He knew how many words, sentences and pages were in every book he read and knew books by heart. He could read a book without opening its covers.

One night he was dreaming or thought he was dreaming that he was as tiny as Tom Thumb, he awoke in great fear, sweating and was astonished to know that he was indeed that small as the storybook character. He was a little terrified, he walked up and down his bed hardly making a dent on the blankets. Am I going to stay like this forever, he thought painfully. Then he had an idea, he went and got the book of Tom Thumb which was now huge and lying on the floor near a chair. With all his might, he opened it and saw the tiny character on the beautifully illustrated page, then he began to resume his size. "Wicked," he muttered and smiled, his fear vanished.

The more Sidney read, the more his imagination expanded. If his parents read anything to him he never had any magical experience.

One early, rainy evening, he was reading comic-books in his room when the room was suddenly invaded by birds, butterflies, snakes, lions, tigers, monkeys, elves, fairies, alligators, hyenas, leopards and rats, all making the same sound in unison which sounded like: "Read! Read! Read! Read! Read!"

His parents banged on his door; his sister was terrified. But when the door was opened, he was the only living thing in his room. There wasn`t feather, fur, hair nor bush anywhere to be seen, in fact Sidney`s room smelt of the sweetest flowers.

One of his favourite books, was, The Town Mouse and the Country Mouse. He had receive it as a birthday present, read it many times, but every time he read it, the story seemed to change : sometimes the town mouse hated the town and wanted to live in the country, and sometimes, the country mouse hated the country and wanted to live in the town. Then a great big ginger cat appeared in the story and said to them: "Don`t be afraid, I won`t harm you. I have a big, lovely house in the country by the seaside. You can stay with me. The sea air is always fresh and clean. You`ll see beautiful butterflies, and birds will sing you to sleep. There are trees with delicious fruits." Of course, the cat was trying to trick them. But then, the mice would agree to go to the country with the cat. And to the cat`s astonishment, on the way, the two mice changed into giant rats, and the ginger cat would scamper off. Then again, the story changed into the town mouse watching television, and the country mouse lying on the grass reading a storybook.

With every change, the mice were in a different country in a different situation.

"I don`t know which is my favourite change in the story. I like them all the same," he said to himself and felt contented.

And after each reading, he heard the mice pattering about his room. Squeaks chimed through his room, coming out into: "Read! Read! Read!" He came down to breakfast one Sunday morning and for a while, he thought his parents and his sister were all mice,or was he in a dream? His face was always shining.

Sidney`s greatest worry was that he was afraid to share this amazing phenomena with anyone or that they would find out about it. After reading at night, before falling off to sleep, he heard many voices and animal noises in his head and room which only he heard. In the morning the voices and noises brought on the new dawn.

He read all the storybooks with or about mice: Mickey Mouse, Mighty Mouse comics, watched Speedy Gonzales cartoons and was enthralled by the magic of mice characters in stories.

From other stories he heard the songs and chatter of the Seven Dwarfs and Snow-white; the wolf huffing and puffing and blowing down houses of the little pigs; the witch shouting at Rapunzel to let down her hair; Rumpeltilskin singing happily that soon he will take the Queen`s child.

He heard and saw the magic of the programmes on children`s television. He turned, moved at the magic of Pinochio. Burped when he heard the Mother Goose Rhymes.

As a toddler and at nursery school, Sidney`s infant mind had probed the Once Upon A time stories. He was always strong and healthy, and continued to grow without any childhood illnesses. His parents found him strange but loved him dearly, even when their second child was born. Sidney and his sister had a nanny sometimes but for most of their childhood, their mother looked after them.

Sidney was never afraid when he first heard and read stories about wicked witches, terrible ogres, dragons breathing fire, werewolves, man-eating crocodiles, lions, tigers growling ferociously. He never cried except as a baby when he was hungry or wanted his nappy changed. His sister found him distant and strange sometimes but she loved him and was proud of him. Everybody thought, what a wonderful child. At primary school he shone with creative intelligence. Sidney was the best at reading and remembering what he read. While Carron was extremely numerate, the best in her class at maths.

Even so, the extent to which Sidney`s imagination carried him, worried his parents, the questions he asked, perplexed them.

He enjoyed everything about Disney even when he was in his mother womb.

Then he began to read, Lord of the Rings by J.R.R. Tolkien, his world expanded further. At first, he thought he could read minds, especially those of his family and friends. Now he thought trolls, elves, fairies and dwarfs were telling him stories. He read the Hobbit first and found a world beyond his everyday existence, his whole being was entirely opened up. Somewhere there was a wizard, a magical storyteller who wrote with word processor who would take him beyond the world around him. He met Tolkien who told him to keep on reading, that a treasure is waiting for him. He read all of Tolkien`s works. He was the brightest pupil at his school, even brighter than the teachers. There wasn`t anything else the school could teach him. He went on to secondary school. He thought that if he tried to learn anything he could do it quite easily and quickly. As he read on, the characters on the pages moved like on a television screen or computer screen. But he was the only one who saw these marvels.

He thought he was being guided and prepared for something extraordinary, and he was taking it step by step. Was he chosen for some higher reading penetration? He tried hard to work it out. Then he began to read J.K.Rowling`s Harry Potter books! And he thought that his head was going to explode! He read all the books quickly and deeply and thought that he was becoming like Harry Potter. He sought the answer in every book: Who was this wizard? This magical storyteller who would take him outside himself to another dimension?

Now a light followed him everywhere, he was the only one who saw the light. Was He becoming a magician? The more he read, the more he felt he was slowly leaving the earth of everyday reality. He felt that if books weren't read, they die. He felt that the characters in the books wanted to come out of the pages and live in the reader`s readers` realities. He wished he could visit Never Never Land and

Alice`s Wonderland! And a voice deep within him always said, "Read! Read! Read more!"

The Princes kept a close eye on their talented son.

One Spring day in early May, Sidney and his two friends were in the back garden of Sidney`s home; they sitting on the soft green grass, talking about boyish things. Sidney looked up at the blue sky with floating bits of white clouds and a flock of birds going by and with a sudden faraway lost, look, said, "I wish I could fly like those birds," his voice was dreamy and gentle.

"That would great if we could all fly like birds and aeroplanes," Ricky .laughed.

"I think reading is great," said Timothy. "You can discover so much about other parts of the world without being there," the three were now looking up at the birds.

The flock of birds squawked loudly. Sidney turned to face Ricky, the strangest look on his face. The other boys were smiling.

"Yes, reading is fantastic," said Timothy.

"Nobody reads like you, Sidney," Ricky said thoughtfully. "You seemed to be lost in the books."

"Aren`t you ever afraid?" asked Ricky, looking intently at Sidney.

"What`s there to be afraid of," Sidney said jokingly, a deep satisfaction moving through his whole body.

A gentle Spring breeze caressed their faces, and the flock of birds disappeared in the distance. Now the sky was cloudless.

"Maybe I might be an author when I grow up," Sidney said reflectively, lying flat on his back, looking at his two friends who seemed to change for a while into characters from the Wizard of Oz and Where the Wild things Are, then the sun came down and sat happily between them.

"Sometimes I have bad dreams whenever I read fairy stories about dragons, witches and giants, " Ricky said drily.

"I get frightened by the wicked behaviour of some storybook people, " Timothy said thoughtfully. "Sometimes I get nightmares. And when I wake up, I remember it`s only a story, it`s not real and can`t be real."

Sidney`s mother called merrily from the opened French-windows, "Would you boys like some refreshments?"

They looked at each other and smiled contentedly and replied together: "Yes, please!" Sidney thrived at High School/Secondary Education. He had read every book children`s book ever written. His mental capacities grew sharper and were second to none. Again, the teachers were simply astonished as he surpassed them in everything. There were wasn`t anything they could teach him. He knew the answers to every question. He passed every test and examination. At thirteen he was ready for university. Now whenever he read, all the words came off the pages and went into his mouth and he absorbed them with a deep breath and fulfilment. Then after a while, he opened his mouth again and the words came out and went back onto the pages. Everyday he went to the library, he joined book clubs, and he also bought books, new and second-hand. Wherever he went he always carried a book, even to the bathroom.

And now he became interested in science fiction and horror novels. He now felt ready for anything. He read books from all over the world. He mastered other languages. And then he began to read Bram Stoker`s Dracula, and became fascinated with all of Stoker`s other stories. Also he was enthralled by Mary Shelley`s Frankenstein, Dr Jekyll and Mr Hyde; books about vampire men and women and books about fantasy and horror. He read all of E.A.Poe every science-fiction book written by H.G.Wells. The written word intrigued him, not what was on television, the movies, computer or radio. He was carried away by the imagination of these writers whom he called "real creative writers", real fiction. He began to understand how the imagination works in the creative artist.

He was the youngest student the university, passed all the exams, becoming top of his class. He attended some of the top universities in the world: Oxford, Harvard, Bologna and Cambridge. And all this time, he never seemed to have a girlfriend or any sexual relationship with a woman or man. It seemed that sex was off his radar. Sidney`s total consciousness was in reading books and going into and living with the stories because he thought that`s where the answers of true fiction lay.

Sidney began to receive signs and signals. He couldn`t understand them at first; it was about this time he began to hear a new voice in his head and dreams. The new voice chanted: "God save the King!" Again "God save the King!" Again and again the voice called. Was it a Royal family in danger? Sidney thought. A King in trouble? Could it be a King in a story? After hearing the voice, and couldn`t understand the meaning, he became weak, his body aching all over and he sweated profusely. It was becoming stranger now, his dreams became as real as waking life. He had to find out who this King was! Maybe it was the ghost of a slaughtered Monarch in a story trying to get his help. Sidney searched the newspapers, he surfed the Net, he searched in books, fiction and non-fiction, he researched into encyclopaedias, but found nothing about a King or Monarch in trouble nor slain.

He asked Ricky and Timothy whom he now hardly saw, but they didn`t know and were busy with girlfriends and further education worries.

The strange voice was male.

Then one night, he was in his room which nowadays he seldom inhabited, deep in thought when he heard a gentle knock on his door: "Come in, " he said softly. The door opened, but no one was there, only a whisper coming through the door like a rush of wind into the room: "God save the King! Long May He Reign! Read the Books!" He snapped out of his thoughts, and thought for a moment that it was Carron but she was out with friends. I have to keep on searching, he thought, his head overflowing with ideas. There must be a story with this King in it, he thought. Who is this King, he racked his brain. He asked lecturers, professors and students at the universities but none were able to help him and none were interested in that kind of fiction.

His father said to him one evening at supper, "Sid, you might be pleased to know that there`s a book, well, a story by an author called, Rudyard Kipling entitled, "The Man Who Would be King". Maybe you should check it out."

"Yes, I`ve heard of it," said Mrs Prince smilingly.

"Me too," said Carron, chewing slowly.

"I`ve checked that story, Dad," Sidney said meekly. "But thanks for looking out for me."

"Well, I don`t know, son," said Mr Prince, sipping a glass of red wine. "I`ll keep a look-out."

Mr Prince had always told his wife that it was so great that his only son loved reading and was so clever. He often boasted to his friends about his son`s achievements.

Mrs Prince shone with pride.

A sunny Sunday in April, the daffodils were in bloom, just before noon, the sun came smilingly through Sidney`s room window which faced the back of the house, the sun kissed him on the lips while he was contemplating a row of books on a shelf. He was thinking of moving out and finding a place of his own. His parents were out. And by now, Carron had a boyfriend and sometimes stayed over at his house. He was wondering if leaving home was a good idea, because although he wanted to be alone sometimes or most of the time, he loved the closeness of his family.

Now everywhere Sidney went, the voice rang in his ear. It was like the National Anthem of Britain, but it wasn`t, it had a different ring to it. He checked on the computer, what about "godsavetheking.com" ??? But it didn`t register. Could it be that in his heightened state of awareness, he was picking up vibrations of a monarch kidnapped somewhere and crying out for help which only he could pick up. And then again, it could be some kind of riddle he had to unravel? Alas, poor Sovereign, he thought deeply and his ear-bells rang.

Sidney was reading very quickly, he was now reading a hundred books a year. His head in stories by Lovecraft which he read and re-read. A monarch in trouble or kidnapped isn`t a problem for him but a problem for a government and its politicians. Still, his imaginative was working beyond over-time. A text rang through his head: "All languages have secrets, the magic is to uncover them. In the supreme light of the imagination, all things are possible. Read on, Sidney! Read on!" Maybe all words have other meanings, other symbols.

The sky glowed with an unbelieveable light, the blue face of heaven burst into a million suns, a very soft bliss kissing Sidney`s face; from amongst the trees birds chanted melodious music and animals danced in a meadow. Sidney was now forcing his imagination into deeper and deeper regions of every book he read. He experienced wonderful, strange new feelings. A text appeared on his mobile-phone: "Mirror, mirror on the wall! Who`s the best storyteller of them all? All writers travel on one journey!" New sounds and colours swam in his brain, merging and separating. It seemed all around him the land was giving birth to magical fruits. Again, another text: "All storytellers must be able to fly! Able to turn the moon into the sun and the sun into a giant moon. Able to make the wind play Mozart and Charlie Parker playing in a band together. Able to blizzards of winter into the hottest summer!". In the night, stars descended and went into his eyes and he became more enlightened. He was beginning to comprehend mysteries of the darkest night. He felt he was a reader destined to uncover the secrets of all the stories in the world.

One winter's night, he was re-reading a Harry Potter book, a moon appeared in his room, hugged and kissed him and J.K.Rowling also appeared, kissed his forehead, whispered in his ear: "Read on, young man." Then she and the moon embraced each other and disappeared

His imagination was beyond the world of books, he had to control it. With a fuller and deeper understanding, he was able to guide the journeys of reading. J.K.Rowling and Tolkien became his guardians, visiting him in dreams, mirrors and visions. When he saw them they came through the faces of his family and friends, and always they said to him: "Read on, go beyond the words and you'll discover much more than the average reader!" He realised he had to discover the great secret all by himself.

Sidney felt that his whole body was being transformed into something of which he knew nothing about, not yet anyway. His head sometimes seemed too heavy on his shoulders. He felt that if he tried to touch the sky he could do so quite easily; his world was an enchanting one. There weren't any boundaries for him. Sometimes he re-read books he read as a child. Now a young man, he blossomed into manhood like the beginning of a new creation. Sometimes in flashes like lightning he saw a word in the sky and it wrapped him into many questions and meanings.

2

It was at Oxford university, Sidney acquired a new friend, his name was William Ripepear who read English and an enthusiastic reader like himself, but William never experienced the deepest passions and magic which Sidney did. They were both at the same college, Oriel. William was very bright but not as bright as Sidney whom he admired greatly. They became friends instantly when they first met and were always together and frequented each other`s homes in the holidays. William was an only child and his parents spoilt him. He had a large library at his home and a small one in his college room. There were books by every English author since Chaucer and also many great European poets, novelists and playwrights. His father was a merchant banker and his mother was a barrister. Their home was a manor house with huge back and front gardens and lots of grounds all around.

On a late June day in late afternoon, William and Sidney were in William`s large and spacious room. Sidney always marvelled at the amount of books at William`s home, he thought at last he had found a kindred spirit.

"They say reading broadens one`s mind," William began, standing near a window near a wall of books. "But I always say, it is the kind of books one reads, that's the essential thing."

"I agree," Sidney smiled, sitting on a stool, looking at his friend. "I like books with magic in them, or books that can open up areas of the imagination undreamt and unheard of. Tales which are not only supernatural but super nature. Books should show other possibilities. I hate surface reality. The author must work very hard for me. He or she must create a new kind of character, a new human being, if you like. Stories must give more than delight. I felt this way even when I was a child. When I read I felt I was growing faster each day. I was so fulfilled, I was getting the greatest satisfaction, I felt like an adult before my time."

"You see, Sid," William sighed deeply, "that`s what stories are about or should be about, magically creating something that`s not of this world. Most novels are about real situations, the writer never seems to work hard for the story or situation. I mean, who wants to know about situations that are already around us." William smiled, his eyes faraway, "Now if I tell you that I met an old man some months ago who gave me a bag of gold and he told me to spend it wisely, to feed, clothe and house the poor and the needy; and then I spend the rest of my life helping the poor and the needy, that wouldn`t be true, not a creative lie, not a creative truth, if you like." Then he opened a book entitled, Tales of the Supernatural, thought for a while, and went on, "But if I told you, I met an old man a month ago and he gave me a bag of gold and told me to spend it wisely to helping the poor and needy, and that if I don`t, all the gold will disappear. I agreed to the old man`s wishes, then before my eyes, the old man disappeared, and the bag of gold also disappeared, why? Why did the bag of gold disappear? Because the old man saw in my mind that I didn`t intend to do what he instructed me, to help the poor and the needy, that I intended to keep the gold all for myself." That`s a creative story, true fiction."

"That`s what I call fantastic!" Sidney rose from the stool, his face shining with appreciation. "That`s the imagination at work at its most creative power. Real and true fiction."

William looked out of the window at the now slowly changing late afternoon, took a deep breath and went, "Creative writing is a skill, a gift, if you like. Being able to create something that has never existed before, is true genius. Well, as far as I am concerned."

Sidney was glowing with radiance, here is someone of my own heart and soul, he thought.

"William faced him again and continued, "You see, the so-called works of fiction that are called great literature, studied in schools, universities and discussed in literary journals and newspapers, aren`t true creative writing. I know many will disagree and want to be-head me but I stand firmly by this belief. The real creative literature is about ghouls, vampires, witches, demons, wolf-men and women and other monsters. Literature which creates something which isn`t in our everyday existence. This creative writer is a real magician; indeed, all artists who create something out of nothing are the true creators."

Sidney was lost for words, he paced the large room, saying, "I see, I see, I see, yes. I`ve read all the fairy stories and a lot of supernatural novels, and was totally convinced that they were the genuine creation inspiration. I felt I was always in another world, indeed, another universe.

William seemed exhausted, lost for words, he staggered, overwhelmed by his own passion.

"I read a hundred books a year," Sidney said without boastful intent.

William looked at him questioningly and blurted, "But.... but...but..that`s what I`d like to achieve. What!" Now he was starry-eyed looking at Sidney as if seeing him for the first time and said, "I know you were capable of something like that. Great! The Harry Potter book s are what real fiction is about. You know, Sid, children have the purest imagination of all. Grown-ups get lost in the mundane world of everyday adult fiction. There is very little real creative adult fiction around."

"Have you ever had the feeling that you were in the story whenever you were reading?" Sidney was thinking that maybe he could trust his friend with his secret, but he trod carefully.

William smiled and said, "But isn`t that how one must read a story!" the exclamation showed that he was being carried along ideas of the unknown.

"Whenever I read I feel I am in the story, actually taking part," Sidney`s voice was firm and serious. I don`t have a wish to be in the tale, I feel I am in the story, however long or short."

"That`s truly startling, truly amazing, my friend, but the wish never comes true, does it?"

William felt suddenly cold. But Sidney was beaming like a sunbeam. "I mean, when one reads, one sets up one`s own pictures of how the characters look, the kind of scenery and so on; like pictures on a screen. Not only the creator of the story, but reader should use his or her imagination to the fullest. Of course, the reader wants to get into the story while they`re reading it, and in way, they`re in it, but that`s only their imagination at work."

Sidney wondered if he should share his secret with this friend who was the only one who came anyway near to what he was feeling and experiencing. Could he trust him? His was a phenomenal insight. And if he did share his secret, what would William think of him! He might be impressed or he might be jealous, or he might think that Sidney was ill and going mad.

"What are you thinking about? You seemed lost in deep thoughts," William`s face softened.

An owl hooted in the vast forest-grounds which neighboured the house. Night came on. Sidney smiled a radiant smile, "Well, I was. I agree with what you were saying, yes," as he was jolted from his reverie.

"It`s all magic writing, Sid," and now William laughed.

A sudden chill ran through Sidney, and deep in his soul he felt something powerful entering his life and would change it for ever. He then, from his eyes, emitted a glow which made William`s eyes popped, his mouth hung open and spittle ran out. "Are you all right, Sid?" he stuttered.

"Oh, yes, I`m feeling fine, never felt better," was the reply, saw the astonishment on his friend`s face and added, "That owl is heralding a remarkable tale, I`m sure."

"Maybe, we`re all part of a magical story," William relaxed as the glow from his friend`s subsided.

"We surely are," Sidney sighed, looked again around William`s library.

On a writingW-table in a corner was computer and printer. "I might try my hand at writing stories as William followed Sidney`s gaze. "Maybe even a novel."

Most of the books in William`s library were about science-fiction, or so-called horror fiction and literary criticism about these books.

Suddenly on the computer screen came on and a name appeared on the screen, like a words he had seen before flashing in the sky.

3

William had done very well at school and university. Women found the two young men weird, most thought that they were lovers, although William had a girlfriend. Sidney`s childhood friends and neighbours had moved to another district. Sidney had lost touch with them .

A tall, slim young woman in her twenties with jet black hair and green eyes and very attractive whom they had met on campus, whose name was Stephanie. All the male eyes were greedily on her, even some of the lecturers and professors. Stephanie walked with her head held very high. She was also bold and had a unbounding tenacity of purpose. She wasn`t as bright as Sidney nor William but had a very keen interest in the same kind of literature as the two young men. William seemed to be the only male who wasn`t dazzled by Stephanie`s beauty, and she knew it and couldn`t understand it.

William was six feet tall and handsome.

"I`ve read some of those books," Stephanie announced one Spring day on campus, coming upon the two young men sitting on a bench, discussing their favourite subject.

She pouted, looking at William intently, "I like Edgar Allan Poe. I think he went deeper than any other American writer. And, my favourite, H.G.Wells` Time machine novel."

Sidney smiled at her.

William`s face was serious but not annoyed by the interruption.

"I don`t think it`s only children should read the Harry Potter books. It`s for adults as well," as she spoke the mid-June sunshine lit up her face.

"Well, yes, that`s very true," said Sidney. "They`re favourites of mine as well. They were extremely clever writing of magical prose.

"Whenever I read I go deeply into the story," she said petulantly. "I become a character in the story, human or animal. And I feel amazingly gratified."

She struck a chord in Sidney`s being, and he said, "Well, everyone reads that way."

William seemed disinterested.

Two men came to them, and Sidney thought : bees attracted by the honey-pot.

William turned his face away.

"Steph, I`d like to hear that CD you were talking about?" asked a medium-sized built man with dirty blond hair, dressed in washed-out jeans and long-sleeved grey shirt and worn-out black and white plimsolls.

"Steph, are you going to town to lunch?" asked the other, a freckled face younger man, dressed in blue dingy corduroy trousers and blue short-sleeved shirt and brown shoes, whose hair was brown.

"Go to your castle, oh, queen," William whispered.

Sidney heard and didn`t mean to giggle.

The two men heard Sidney`s giggle.

Stephanie frowned, long-faced and went off with her two admirers following.

"She thinks she`s God`s gift to men," William said sternly, looking up at a bright blue and thinking, that it was much more beautiful than Stephanie.

"Why don`t you like her. I mean, she`s into what we`re into," Sidney was smiling. "She doesn`t mean any harm really. She can`t help being very pretty."

"I know, but I think she`s very self-centred, that`s all. I don`t hate her." William shrugged, I think she`s a show-off. Let`s change the subject."

And they resumed the discussion about the magical art of story writing. But Sidney sensed there was something more about Stephanie that William didn`t want to talk about.

He had a strange feeling in the pith of his stomach; Stephanie was like a character from a story he had read, not evil but mysterious, he wondered if William detected it or did he suspect it?? His face became clouded.

Stephanie began to be drawn towards Sidney and William in ways she didn`t understand. At first, William didn`t trust her, but he slowly understood her attraction to them . Whenever she spoke to them, her face always lit up like a Christmas tree. She thought the three of them had everything in common.

There was a rumour going on that Stephanie never went to the toilet. It sounded incredible to Sidney and

William when they heard it. And she seemed to revel in the rumour because she thought that it made her cleaner and more beautiful. William thought it was all nonsense spread by Stephanie herself.

Whenever Sidney looked into her eyes, he detected a strange animal instinct, a non-human sensation. But how was that possible, he thought, is she hiding something from us and the world.

One early autumn day, the three of them were in Sidney's room at college, a fart broke the silence as they were contemplating books. Sidney couldn't believe his sense of smell as Stephanie said, "Sorry". When the scent reached his nostrils, it was the sweetest perfume he had ever smelt. William looked at him quizzically as they stared at each other. How could that be? They thought together.

"We are going to be the best of friends," she beamed, looking at them with a wide smile, her voice was soothing. "We are special." And she farted again, louder than before, this time the smell perfumed the entire room and went through an open window. "I beg your pardon!" she intoned merrily as a streak of sunlight came through the window maybe somewhat refreshed by the perfumed wind.

Sidney didn't see Stephanie for a long time after this episode. He wondered where she was and was she embarrassed and avoiding their company. Or was she ill? William was somewhat relieved. She was indeed an unusual person.

"She's probably have a very bad period," William said haphazardly.

"It`s a long time to have a period," Sidney wondered what kind of a period a woman like Stephanie was having.

In late July, the sky was overcast, Sidney and William were taking a walk around William`s family estate with stately oaks, pine trees, cherry-blossoms, forget-me-nots, elms and silver birch, when a sudden wind wrapped around them like a blanket. They hurried to the house.

William was sarcastic, "Oh, I`ve been thinking about the fart and the perfumed smell and Stephanie never going to the toilet. And, all I can say is, that there are some strange human beings in this world, maybe she`s one of those. I don`t know what to think about her anymore."

The sky became clear. The wind subsided.

"Stephanie is certainly not like any woman I`ve ever met," Sidney said breathlessly. "And then Again, it could be all in our minds after all the books we`ve been reading. Some people might even say we`re imagining and hallucinating."

"I know for a fact, I wasn`t hallucinating," said William sharply. "Some people will say and do anything to gain the attention and admiration of others. Remember we`re in the age of celebrity status. Everybody wants` to be famous or special."

"I saw a programme on television a week ago about extraordinary people with deformed bodies, unusual limbs growing on their bodies and strange bodily functions."

"Yes, but how do they shit and piss with perfumed smells!" William laughed.

And they both laughed all the way to the house.

When they arrived, Sidney went quickly to the toilet and urinated for a long time, as he did so, he was filled with thoughts of Stephanie, she was very beautiful indeed, but equally very mysterious. He felt tired whenever he thought of her as if he was being drained just thinking of her. After a long session with William, he went to bed late into the morning and dreamt of Stephanie.

The holidays summer holidays enchanted him, spending them with William.

4

Sidney`s tutor, a short, balding man with bright curious blue eyes, always in pin-striped blue suit, had a name Sidney found strange, Dr Nehpets. Sidney was going to find out something startling about that name later on. Although Dr Nehpets` features were that of the Northern European, his name suggested to Sidney other associations; he spoke with a upper middle-class English accent. Dr Nehpets was fascinated by Sidney. Nehpets had three Ph.D.s, two were from Harvard and Yale respectively and the other from Cambridge. He had the same literary interests as Sidney. He also had an interest in conventional English and American literature. His preference was for the supernatural and fantasy.

At his book-crammed, spacious study, he asked Sidney one late autumn day, "My dear, Mr Prince, you very wise to choose such literature. I have a craving for it myself."

Sidney felt completely relaxed, looking at some of the titles on the shelves, his response was profound, "Sir, I believe, ever since I was a child, that so-called supernatural, horror and fantasy, are the true fiction, I mean, real creative writing.

Nehpets` eyes became curiouser than ever, seeming to penetrate the young man. "But are you rejecting other literatures?" Nehpets was in his fifties but his face suddenly seemed much younger.

Sidney, sighed, smiled and looking intently at his tutor, replied, "Sir, it`s use of the imagination. Creating something that isn`t in this world. It`s the power to create, the power to invent a new character, a new life." And he got carried by his own enthusiasm, "Now, let`s take, War and Peace", the novel tells us about history, specifically, European history, European life. Tolstoy`s imagination wasn`t working very hard because European history was already laid out before him. It was easy for him to move events and people around because they were already extant. It is great historical writing, brilliantly done, but for me, not creative writing. Now when you come to a novel like Mary Shelley`s Frankenstein, there you have a work of pure creativity, because the author had created something out of nothing, if you like. I can cite other works, Dracula, Wells` War of the Worlds, Oscar Wilde`s Dorian Gray and Dickens` A Christmas Carol and many others of this ilk of which you`re no doubt aware." As he spoke, his face shone.

Nehpets surveyed Sidney`s face carefully and said, "I understand exactly what you`re saying young man. I`ve been thinking about this for a very long time, in fact when I was your age. Academics and critics must pay close attention to the kind of literature you and I are interested in. They call it fantasy writing. All fiction is fantasy. Fantasy is the more imaginative. Most of human history is horror anyway."

Sidney was bathing in the glory of Nehpets` words. "For me when I read it I feel a higher state of consciousness. I seem to go outside myself.

Dr Nehpets sitting at his desk with books, papers, computer, his mobile-phone and cup-and-saucer, was overwhelmed by Sidney`s words, he seemed almost hypnotised.

"When I read, I enter the story," Sidney went on. "Not only mentally, but physically too. I`m taking part in the story."

"You`re a dynamic student, Mr Prince," Nehpets said soothingly, "the brightest I`ve ever had. What you`re saying is quite fantastic and revolutionary. There are many people, most of them readers, who will say you`re only hallucinating and on drugs. Critics and most academics will think you`re insane." And now he was smiling widely with his entire face. Have you told anybody else about this?"

"Only one friend who`s also here reading English," Sidney replied.

"How are you getting on otherwise with university life?" Nehpets was still smiling.

"I find the experience demanding at times, but I have no insurmountable problem,"

Nehpets had the deepest respect and admiration for the young man, whenever he spoke to him he experienced refreshing of his mind. Sidney was his favourite student.

One bright Saturday in mid-August, Sidney met William for lunch in town. The sun shone brilliantly on their faces as they sat outside on the pavement of the restaurant. The waitress came and both of them ordered a tuna-salad, potatoes and a glass of white wine. They both thought the food was divine and ate hungrily.

Suddenly, a shrill laugh was heard, both of them recognised it as coming from none other than Stephanie. They looked at each other quizzically and then in the direction of Stephanie who was smiling and wearing a summery bright flowered dress, white sandals; her hair tied in a pony-tail; she headed straight to their table.

"What! And to think I was just thinking about her," William spat out some of his food.

"Me too," Sidney said and he stopped eating.

"I was also thinking of the both of you," Stephanie said merrily. "Maybe we`re on the same wave-length."

Sidney stared unblinkingly at her and chewing slowly.

William wiped his mouth then sipped his glass.

"Mind if I join you," said Stephanie as she pulled up a chair. "That salad looks delicious and I`m famished."

"Yes, sure, yes!" said Sidney.

William made a little nod.

They both were surveying her, undressing her with their eyes.

Stephanie signalled the waitress, a pretty slim young woman, and she ordered a tunasalad. She was smiling all the time. She was wearing a lot of make-up, ear-rings of pearls and a silver chain which sparkled with the rays of the sunlight.

"Long time, no see. How are you?" Sidney enquired, sipping, his eyes twinkling, probing,

"I`m fine, Sid," she beamed, her eyes flashing. "And how is your faithful friend, William?"

"We are well, they replied together.

Sidney sipped. William poured out some more wine, both kept looking at Stephanie.

"Would you like some wine?" they both asked her.

"No, thank you, just a glass of water," Stephanie answered. "I`m taking life one step at a time. Whatever life throws at me, I`m dealing with it the best way I can. Life is too short to over exert one`s self with worry." Now she was looking only at Sidney.

William sighed heavily, rose and said, "Excuse me, I`m afraid Nature calls." And he went off to a gents toilet.

Stephanie studied William`s back as he went off.

The waitress came again, smiling and busy.

"I`d like the same as these two gentlemen, please, and a glass of water," Stephanie smiled. Then the smile disappeared from her face and a faraway look appeared. "I`ve been thinking about going on an adventure," now her tone was dreamily. "Where to, I haven`t yet decided. But I was thinking maybe the three of us could go. The idea crept into my head a week ago."

Sidney thought it was a good idea. "Of course, we`ll have to ask Will."

Suddenly the bright sunshine dipped, the sky and surroundings darkened. Faces went sullen. Light rain began to spit, then to a shower in large drops like hail-stones which people thought at first they were. The rain was now heavy.

"Oh, God, it`s going to ruin the food!" said Stephanie disappointedly.

Sidney, Stephanie and the customers outside now rushed into the restaurant.

"Anyway, I`ve lost my appetite, and William`s food is ruined," Stephanie went on.

"We were finished anyway, there`s hardly anything there," said Sidney. "I'll have what`s left of the wine. We can order more food and more wine."

"No, it`s all right," Stephanie said contentedly, "I`ll just have some water. When William comes back we can talk about my idea of an adventure."

When they were inside and sitting at a table in a corner, Sidney shrugged and said, "Yes, well, I`ve lost my appetite as well. Let`s see what Will has to say, eh."

"All right," Stephanie muttered, looking around.

William came straight to them as if guided by a radar and said, "The rain has put me off food."

The rain stopped, the sky brightened and birds sang in nearby trees.

"English weather is sometimes magical," Stephanie said, turning to William as he sat down, then asked, "Would you like to come on an adventure with us. I mean, Sidney, you and I. Are you game for it?"

William looked at her strangely and answered, "Yes, I am game for an adventure." And he looked at Sidney who nodded.

Some of the customers returned to sit outside. The three remained in the corner.

Mobiles rang!

Shafts of sunlight were coming through windows, glass and door of the restaurant.

"William, it`s an adventure I`ve had in mind for a long time," Stephanie began slowly. "How about us three going on a trip. Of course, in the holidays. What do you think?"

William thought for a while, then said, "Sounds very interesting ."

"I think it could be a voyage of self-discovery," Sidney put in, looking intently at William.

Sidney didn`t carry on, because his mobile rang, he was waiting for a special call, "Excuse me," he said to Stephanie and William and tuned aside. He didn`t recognise the voice.

"Don`t be surprised nor shocked, Mr Prince," the voice said kindly. "And don`t be afraid. I mean you no harm. King isn`t going to lead you astray. You are going to show the literary world what real creative writing is . You can say I`m the voice of the real book of fiction. I`m so glad someone like you came along," the voice was soothing. Sidney thought it was a prank call, or one of the characters from a story getting through to him. He had many pictures in his head.

"Now, I must go. I can hear you`re confused," the caller`s voice solemnly continued. "Read me. Don`t let anyone tell you otherwise. Keep reading strong."And the voice faded away.

"Hello! Hello!" Sidney called out. As William and Stephanie watched each other and watched him, startled.

"No, don`t hang up! Wait! Who! Where!" I bet it`s that King business again, he thought, his face glowing more than ever.

"Sid, that happens all the time on phone and computers," said Stephanie. "It`s a prankster. Some people have a lot of time to waste."

William nodded, "Yes, the other night someone called on my mobile and told me if I`d like to have eternal life. I wonder how they get our phone-numbers. There are a lot of identity-thieves around. We must ever be on our guard."

Then a voice spoke in Sidney`s ear which only he heard, "It`s me. I`m no prankster. I`m Stephen King. It`s time to read me." Then his ear popped. He looked at his two friends a little dismayed. "My ear-bell just popped ", he said, cleared his throat and said, "Yes, about that journey. I`m sure it`s going to be a great one.

They spoke and planned the trip around the world. Sidney knew that his journey was going to have something to do with this King character. At a library one day, he noticed a book entitled, Carrie by Stephen King, an American novelist. He flicked through the pages and as he did so, he felt a shiver through his whole body.

This must be the writer I have to read, he thought and then he felt tremendously relieved, as if a great burden was lifted from his shoulders, a great reading problem was solved. He felt that if he tried to fly and walk on water he could accomplish these feats. He had never felt this way before, he was in another world. I am sure now that this is the writer who is trying to contact me. He must have a very powerful imagination to get to me this way. He felt the greatest surge in his body and soul, filled with the great spirit, the greatest motivation. Stephen King, I`m going

to read everything you`ve written. He cuddled the novel
which was in hardback and heard voices coming from the
pages: "Read and understand me!" he heard a gentle voice
saying above all the others. And he answered, "Yes! Yes!
Yes! I`ll read you!"

5

Sidney began to read Stephen King`s novels and stories, and he realised a whole new meaning of creative writing; this was the author he was searching for all his life. All the voices and apparitions he was hearing were guiding him to Stephen King, a giant of an author, indeed, a King. His whole life changed, not just his reading. His imagination was opened up a hundredfold. His senses became more acute; his brain power was now much brighter than before, on par with Einstein and Da Vinci. Now he felt he was more clever than Professors, critics and inventtors. He was beginning to be hailed as a genius. He saw creative literature in new light. He already thought that real creative writing was written by authors who created something that didn`t exist; they were almost God-like. His brain was working at the fullest capacity.

It was like Spring was forever in the air as he devoured the works of Stephen King. The voice that was now speaking to him was caring, fatherly and totally sure of itself. "God Save the King", he uttered and it felt sweet in his mouth.

"Now you`re ready, Sidney Prince," the voice chanted in his deepest consciousness and in his dreams. "You`re ready!" And he seemed to sail away light-years from earth.

He read King`s works slowly and carefully, making notes and underlining sentences, words and paragraphs. He was joyful, and felt he not only he must read King`s works, he must meet him in the flesh.

As he read the novel, Carrie, he wondered if he could move objects by the power of his now very powerful mind. He tried but was unsuccessful. Maybe he wasn`t concentrating hard enough. As he went deeper into the novel, he felt his chest expanding, his heart like a great drum and a tremendous warmth enveloping his being and he felt a great sense of joy and satisfaction. He entered the novel and the characters were waving at, touching him, shaking his hand. Then Carrie herself, was smiling and hugged him. And a halo came over his head.

"Who`s that?" Carrie`s mother appeared and bellowed. "I bet he`s after your virginity!"

Sidney smiled, "No, Ma`am, I love to read and I love Stephen King`s stories, and they have led me here. I mean no harm to any of you."

"Such a silver tongue for one so young," the mother snapped.

Carrie winked, and now only she and Sidney were together in a meadow.

"Tell me," she began, her voice gentle and sweet. "How did you really get here?"

Sidney was still smiling, "I`m sure someone like you will understand and believe me. You see, I love to read and listen to stories ever since I was a child. I love stories about magic and the supernatural. The more I read, the more I became more clever at school and university. I was clever at home and with my friends. You can move objects with the power of your mind. I am able to do things with the power of my reading. And now, reading the author of this novel I can enter his stories. It`s wonderful to be here. That`s the truth."

Carrie looked at him carefully, saying, "You`re English, aren`t you? You`re sure this isn`t some kind of trick?"

"Yes, I`m English. And I assure you, Miss Carrie, this is no trick I`m trying to put over on you . It`s the honest truth." Sidney stopped smiling, his face was now serious. "The man who wrote this story which you`re the main character, is called Stephen King. Somehow I was guided by forces to read his work. It wasn`t until I was ready that his stories were revealed to me. Now he`s the only author I read. They call his stories, horror, but I think his stories are real creative fiction, real art. You were his first full length novel to make him into a success .No other writer of this kind of fiction is as good as him. None of them woke me up to this great thrill, excitement, and satisfaction."

"Are you telling me that I`m the figment of somebody`s imagination?" Carrie`s face was now forlorn and there was a strange light in her eyes. "Do you mean, he`s like God?"

"No, he`s a King. Indeed, a King of writers," Sidney said matter-of-factly. "He`s an artist who goes beyond everyday existence. He shows the possibilities of the imagination.

The vision of Carrie in the sunlit meadow suddenly disappeared, and Sidney found himself on the university campus near a door of a building where Dr Nehpets was giving a seminar.

"What is quite remarkable," Dr Nehpets was saying, "is that a lot of what Prince is saying make sense. His ideas, his essays make sense. I can see moments in the novel, Dracula where there is a reversal of conventional reality.............."

Sidney`s entire being smiled, he was experiencing bodily changes. Was he becoming one of Stephen King`s characters? he thought . He was now seeing through walls, and could hear speech and other sounds from great distances. But he couldn`t fly nor walk on water. He didn`t know what to think of Dr Nehpets. He developed skills in other areas: he could play any musical instrument and any composition; he could paint beautiful pictures. Doctors and psychologists couldn`t understand this phenomenon. Before reading Stephen King he had never showed any inclination to music nor painting.

His parents were dumbfounded. When asked, all they said was, as a child all he loved was listening to stories and reading.

Sidney felt deep within himself that he was supposed to go on a quest, not the journey Stephanie had suggested. But a search, but in search of what? He didn`t know at the present Time. He also knew that it would come to him, he had to be patient.

He read and read and went deeper into King`s books. He was waiting for the call. Sometimes he met Carrie and he wasn`t surprised nor shocked but captivated in her: Sometimes she was at his home or at his college, or they were in a park enjoying a Spring or summer sunshine, and she always said, "With King everything in stories are possible", then she would kiss him and return to the novel. She was always loving and inspired his movements.

Early one autumn evening with a cloudy sky and a sultry moon moving through the darkness and a wind rustling surroundings trees, Sidney met a gnarled old man sitting on a bench in a park.

"Good evening, young man!" the old man greeted him politely. "My name is Yucross!"

Sidney`s eyes were penetrating and questioning. "Good evening to you. And my name is Sidney Prince. And what can I do for you?"

After the bright sparkle his greeting, Yucross` eyes and face lost some of their glow. And The sky and surroundings became darker, winds now swayed the trees.

"It looks like we`re in for an autumn storm, eh" Yucross tried to brighten up but failed.

There was Something about Yucross Sidney didn`t understand, he seemed false, in disguise, and he felt Yucross knew about his suspicions. Sidney looked around, trying to penetrate the darkness, then he looked again at Yucross, held up a hand and said, "Who are you really?"

Yucross became agitated, uncomfortable and angry.

Sidney sensed it and said, "Why are you angry? Forgive me if I offend you."

The weather now worsened: the sky was black, winds howled and rain spat. But Sidney was comfortable and unmoved in his over-coat and fur hat, "You can tell me anything. I won`t be afraid nor angry. Whatever you have to tell me. I`m ready to hear it." His voice clear and precise.

Yucross looked extremely ruffled, looking around wildly, saying "My, my, the weather is changing all the time."

"Well, I`m a reader," Sidney began. "I love reading a writer named Stephen King. He`s the king of writers as far as I`m concerned." his voice was strong and commanding.

"I think all stories.....stories.....are.....I.....have......stor....." Yucross seemed lost for the right words. He looked around suddenly, searchingly as if was lost and seeing everything for the first time.

"King is the writer we all should read," Sidney went on as if he was giving a sermon. "His readership is one of the largest in the world. He`s very, very serious about his work. I can`t understand why he hasn`t been given the Nobel Prize for literature."

"I don`t......know...I......I...but....but.....I....am here....I...." Yucross dribbled all over the front of his black over-coat.

The weather suddenly brightened. The moon smiled through departing dark clouds and upon the faces of the two men.

"I ask you again, who are you? Do you have something for me?" Sidney was forceful. "I know you`ve been following me around for a long time. Are you spying on me?"

"I don`t know what you are talking about, young man," Yucross stuttered, cringed, his whole body was shaking.

"Have been sent to stop me from reading King and taking him seriously? Are you one of those critics who undermines King`s work? If so, you are all going to fail. No! No! You don`t know what true creative literature is about. It`s about the imagination working at full stretch."

"I`m no critic nor academic," Yucross muttered, then squirmed. "I`m a musician. I heard you playing the piano one day, you play Brahms so beautifully, I felt I had to meet you. I love Brahms very much. And you seem to reveal the true Brahms when you play. And I wanted to know how could that be. I think it`s like listening to Brahms. I thought you were the ghost of my beloved Brahms or some kind of magician."

"Why are you in discomfort? " Sidney was sharp. "Am I terrible?"

"No, it`s not that, it`s .... you see.... I was a great concert pianist....and ....I had....a....a terrible accident....a collision.... our car was totally destroyed....our bodies were shattered to pieces.....hardly identifiable.......I......I....died....I`m....dead......"

"I suspected you might be some kind of ghost," Sidney was still in complete possession of his faculties.

"Your reading of Stephen King which gave you great power to play Brahms so magnificently, has resurrected me. I`m alive again. And at first I thought a jealous person- and there were quite a few - had hired a sorcerer to torture, kill me and then I'll return as a restless spirit without a soul to roam the earth. Now I know that isn`t true. You can see me, we can converse. Your tone and manner are kind. And your Brahms is like mine. Hail this Stephen King! Now I can rest in peace. Thanks to you and the King. I think one day King will achieve the Nobel Prize. To hell with his critics. I`ve crossed many rivers and seas in my journey to you, Mr Prince. Love, peace and happiness to you and your quest." And Yucross vanished. And Sidney heard the music of Brahms all around the deserted park.

Carrie appeared, and said, "That was a great meeting. But I must warn you. Be on your guard. There are literary critics employing evil forces to ruin King; they are jealous of his international sales and reputation. Maybe these critics are the evil beings in all stories. But remember not all literary critics are evil-doers." And Carrie disappeared.

Sidney sat on the bench and pondered all.

"The adjudicators and promoters of the Nobel Prize believe that they know about great literature, but the eyes, hearts and minds must be opened to what is real imaginative power in fiction," he said to himself and he heard Carrie`s voice, chanting, Hail the King!"

Sidney thought he was now beginning to understand the magical workings of Stephen`s mind. He thought of writing a book about King, not an academic one and not a critique of King`s work .A book which will go deeper than a devoted fan`s great love for King`s work. He felt that everything was in King`s work, and wherever it leads him he`s going to follow. His life was now in the hands of Stephen King and he felt he was going to be re-born with the pen of King or better still, The King.

6

He didn`t read King`s books in the order in which they were written and published. He was enthralled and completely under the spell of Carrie. He read the novel five times, it flowed into his soul. Carrie taught him many things, to see through people who are false, watch out for fiendish critics who sought the ruination of King and avoid accidents. "These fiendish critics think King is a trash writer", saying these words upset Carrie. Sidney too was upset. "But of course, they wrong. King has brought us together. I fee l more than justa character in a novel. I feel free as a bird. With King the is an amazing place. You`ve gonefurther than any reader of King`s works. Take care of yourself." And Carrie vanished.

Sidney felt a great and powerful love for Carrie and that love lifted him beyond the everyday life. He kept all these things to himself for the present time. On two occasions he thought of meeting King, he wrote to him but got no response: he`s too busy writing, I won`t bother him. My job is to read and study him. I`ll meet him in the pages, he thought. His mission was to herald Stephen King as one of the most gifted writers in the world. He was to try to influence everyone that Stephen King was a prospective Nobel Prize Winner. All kinds of thoughts raced through his mind, and the main one was: why wasn`t King taken as seriously as T.S. Eliot. He had become extremely audacious since he began reading Stephen King. Carrie`s words always echoed in his mind, "Be careful!

Sidney went all over America. He met a fat middle-aged lady in Maine. It was a strange meeting: she came up to him in the street and said, "Young man, I saw you on the Internet."

Sidney wasn`t surprised, because strange things were now an occupational hazard and more so now he was in Stephen King`s country.

The woman`s voice was cheerful. She smiled, looked around at the chestnut tree-lined late Spring street, then suddenly her face took on a sad aspect, her hands trembled.

Sidney felt he had encountered this woman somewhere before.

"Oh, I love King`s work," she said and her whole body shook whilst she spoke.

Sidney felt thunder in his chest.

They walked slowly, and she pointed out the various locations of which King put in his novels and stories. They both seemed to move quickly although they were walking slowly.

"You and I are kindred spirits," her voice was dreamy, looking at a library building. "My husband died some years ago. He was killed in an automobile accident in Paris. He was, what they call, an oil magnate. We were very much in love when we got married." Her voice was faraway, tears surfaced and ran down her cheeks. "His name was Bruce. And, by the way, I`m Mabel."

"Please, you don`t have to tell me, if it upsets you," Sidney felt her sorrow.

"Bruce`s car was going along at a reasonable speed, and a drunk driver crashed into his car. He and his chauffeur were killed instantly." Mabel carried, voice weakening. "I love the name, BRUCE, it`s like soothing and all-inspiring music to me whenever I say it, BRUCE. The sound of the name always relieves my pains, grief and sadness, Bruce, Bruce." And she thus brightened.

Sidney stopped. They were near a bridge. Mabel looked down at the river and her body relaxed, she felt contentment.

"After that terrible tragedy," she continued, "I promised myself, I`d never get married again. I`ve never met anyone like Bruce. I`ve never loved anyone nor anything as I loved my beloved Bruce that includes my parents and two brothers."

"That`s so sad," and Sidney`s voice trembled as he felt her intense pain.

"That`s very kind and considerate of you, Mr Prince." Mabel seemed to be lifted and her face took on a glow. "Bruce left everything to me. We had no children. We tried and tried but weren`t successful. I`m a very rich woman. But I feel in losing Bruce, I have nothing." And she looked away. "Then I started reading Stephen King, and a weird thing began to happen to me." She stopped and looked down at the river with slight breeze rippling its surface.

Sidney felt a great upheaval in his stomach, a kind of awakening.

They walked on. The slight breeze left it`s rippling of the river`s surface and gently caressed their faces.

"I think this State is the most intriguing of the New England States, and Bruce loved it," Mabel blushed.

Sidney thrilled and agreed, "Yes, I think so too," his face glowed.

"Well, let`s journey to Bangor, eh," Mabel said happily. "And although on foot, we`ll move as if we are powered by a jet engine. And all because we read Stephen King deeply and we`re in his birth-place." Her voice had a melodious ring.

They moved magically as if teleported away through space and time. Mabel was relaxed and said, "One June night, I was lying on my bed reading, Salem`s Lot. I was alone in the house which was a grand house like a castle. I thought I heard someone or something enter the bedroom. I didn`t see anything. I just had a deep consciousness that someone had come through the door. My bedroom was at the top floor of the house which has seven floors. I thought, could it be that I was so completely engrossed in the novel, I didn`t see anyone enter? My bedroom is very large with wall-to-wall cupboards, closets and shelves. I became frightened. Maybe a burglar came in unnoticed and is hiding in a closet, I thought. I picked up my mobile which was on a bedside table but before I could dial the police.................." She stopped and looked around as if lost.

"It`s all right, you don`t have to tell me if the memory makes you unhappy," said Sidney soothingly.

They heard music in the distance, rock-and-roll music which delighted them.

"As I was saying," Mabel took a deep breath and continued. "Before I could phone the police, I heard Bruce`s voice. It was clear and enchanting as on the day we first met.

Sidney felt a great surge in the pit of his stomach, now winds in the surrounding trees hummed his name. Could it be that Mabel was experiencing the same magical things as him, after reading King? His mind flooded with magical thoughts as they moved through Maine. They were enchanting thoughts.

"Are you all right?" Mabel touched his arm.

"Yes, yes, I`m fine," and he wondered he should tell Mabel about his magical experiences since he started read King. She certainly wouldn`t think he was mad or delusional if she washaving similar experiences? He wanted to hear more of her experiences.

"Did you speak to Bruce`s ghost?" he asked, firmly but gently with a twinkle in his eye.

"Well, at first, I thought I was hallucinating or dreaming," Mabel`s voice became unsteady.

"But our love had always given us a tremendous bond stronger than anything else in our lives. I knew in my soul that it was Bruce. I felt him."

Sidney overflowed with belief and excitement, his entire body was smiling.

And now they were in Bangor. They both looked around and felt they knew this place, it was in their waking and dreaming lives. They also felt beyond the world.

"Bruce's ghost appeared again," Mabel's face emitted a golden light. "I was reading The Dead Zone. And it was then I realised that these ghostly, visionary experiences were happening because I was reading Stephen King."

Sidney felt a triumph. He knew it. He was over the moon with joy. Indeed, all the light of the fullest moon shone in his soul.

"Bruce appeared, in solid physical flesh. I was reading King everyday like prayers. And then one night, Bruce was on the bed with me, we were making love passionately as ever. From then on, I knew God had sent Stephen King's stories into my life. So for me, Bruce isn't dead, lives for me as long as I read King. I know someone like you, Mr Prince will believe me."

"I do believe you, Mabel, and it's Sidney, please, not Mr Prince," Sidney was beaming. " We are on the same journey. That's fact. Bruce lives."

"Everyday and night, he comes to me," Mabel swooned, and her face looked years younger. "He's having a second life with me. And I'm the only one who can see him. I love it that way."

Along Maine's dramatic coastline, they came to Acadia National Park and breathed in the spectacular mountains and ocean panoramas. And Mabel was becoming a young woman in her twenties. Sidney felt all the vibrations coming out of her young body, "Oh,Mabel," he was consumed with admiration and they embraced tightly.

"Yes, reading King and being in his place of birth and youth, I can be whatever I want to be and wherever I want to be," she said merrily.

"I know, Mabel, I know," he said gently. "And nothing can harm nor frighten you. I have some magical experiences myself. You know, King may never win the Nobel Prize, so what. He sells more books and is more popular than any of the laureates in the 20th century. Most people don`t know who is the current Nobel laureate. A book is published to be read, and when it is read by millions, it is appreciated and successful. Readers determine the brilliance and genius of a writer. When a book is hardly read, it means the writer is sick, when it is not heard of, it means the writer is dead."

"Well, Sidney," Mabel said happily. "No one can prevent his world-wide readership. I`m sure there are readers like us."

Suddenly, all around and in the distance, voices began to chant : "Stephen! Stephen! Master of creative fiction! Stephen remakes the world from here and into everywhere! The King reigns! Come into the life of the main man!"

"There are evil ones about trying to physically hurt Stephen, you know," Mabel was stern, her face sad.

"Oh,I know, I know," Sidney spoke quickly. He felt that Mabel was becoming another woman, another awareness of the situation. "Do you remember in the novel, MISERY, there`s a writer who has been kidnapped by a zealous fan: this can happen to King. I believe therein lies the key to unlocking a secret. I`ve read the novel three times."

"Yes, I understand. I read the novel twice," Mabel agreed.

They were now in Portland, walking through the old district to the area where King was born. They saw an image of his uncle dowsing for water with the bough of an apple-tree branch. They felt a great lift and began to levitate and frightened some passersby, so they decided to be invisible until they were out of sight of the frightened passersby, then they became visible again.

A young woman with a book in her hand approached them, the book was King`s book on writing.

"First they said he had an accident while taking a walk. Then they said, he was kidnapped!" the young woman was distraught, trembled as she spoke. "Stephen King! Stephen King.....they.....kidnappppppp....ed.....he`s .....in an accccccidddent!" she stuttered and almost fell over. Sidney supported her up.

"Oh, my God, it has happened!" Sidney and Mabel said together.

"The writer...Ki...ng.....Ste..ph...en.... Stephen.......King," the young woman moaned, holding up the copy in front of her face.

Sidney and Mabel knew the book, he felt weak at the knees.

Mabel`s stomach ached.

"So that`s it, eh," Sidney said his face taking on a new brightness. "Cursed spite, I was born to put it right. That`s the journey I have to take. That`s the secret I have to uncover."

"It was on television, radio and in the local and national newspapers," the young woman seemed to lose her bearings, turned, pouting and went off angrily.

"I`ll help you in your quest, if you`ll permit me to," Mabel said. "It`s so great meeting you."

They felt an electric charge surging through their bodies. Their faces lit up like light bulbs.

"I think I`m going to meet more characters from King`s stories soon, they`ll have clues as to where the kidnappers are keeping him.

"You are a remarkable human being," Mabel said, her eyes sparkling.

"Of course, I`d like you to accompany me on my quest," Sidney said confidently.

"But.....but....wait.....I hear a voice...calling...me....what.... it`s .. it`s...Br...uce...Bruce....I`m so sorry I can`t come with you, Sidney. But, good luck. Find our beloved, Stephen King." And slowly Mabel disappeared before Sidney`s eyes.

Sidney smiled and surveyed Maine: he went to the Maine State House, the picturesque water-way, the coast, the forested interior, Maine State Parks, Bubble Rock, Saint John River valley area; tasted its seafood, saw Mt Washington Scenic Drives, Bar Harbor, and to the University of Maine Fogler library. He searched, soaking up all the areas where he thought King would`ve been. He felt the presence of King inside him, willing him on.

7

Sidney was soaked in Stephen King`s birth-place. He saw moose, the Katahdin woods and waters, the jagged rocky coast line, the low, rolling mountains, stately oaks, and he spent a long time in Augusta. In Bangor he was transported to another dimension. Now he felt King was with him like an aura around him. Now, he must be on the trail of those kidnappers!

Could it be that King was kidnapped by adoring readers like in his novel, MISERY? Then he thought of the most evil character in King`s works, The Crimson King. Could he have come out of the stories and kidnapped King to get him to re-write the stories in the Crimson`s favour? But he still thought that it was a jealous critic. Or maybe they are both in it together.

Sidney decided to begin his search in those stories where the Crimson appeared. He was back in England. On a bright sunny early afternoon in August, he was walking along a side-street in London near Hyde Park, he bumped into his friend William.

"Hello Sid, old chap!" William rushed to him, they embraced, "long no see!"

"How are you, Will?" Sidney beamed a bright light penetrating William`s face.

"I`m fine, old friend," Will looked at Sidney, searchingly from head to feet. "Where have you been? I`ve been hearing some astonishing things about you . I wonder if it was the same Sidney Prince."

"I`ve been in America," Sidney smiled. "I`m doing some research on the American writer Stephen King, you know."

"Oh, yes, I know his work, of course," William said happily.

The sky was blue and cloudless, a ray of sun crossed Sidney`s face and he raised a hand to shield his face. A nightingale called from a nearby tree and looked in that direction.

"Let`s go and have a drink or something?" William suggested merrily.

"Sure, yes," Sidney replied. And they walked away.

"I hope I`m not keeping you from a prior engagement?" William said.

"Well, yes, but there`s always time for an old friend, it`s all right," Sidney beamed as they approached a café.

"I know that writer, Stephen King became a favourite of yours," William said.

They went, sat at a table inside and ordered two beers. As they sipped, William was very curious.

Sidney couldn`t remember telling William about Stephen King was his favourite author. "Yes, Stephen King is now the only one I`m reading."

"Are you planning post-graduate studies on him?" William asked between sips.

"Maybe, yes, I`m still working on some ideas," Sidney didn`t want to disclose anything to anyone even William.

"Well, I don`t know if you`ve heard, I saw in an item of news somewhere, it said that King was taking a walk in a country lane and was hit by a van or truck, I can`t remember exactly," William`s voice wavered.

A shadow came over Sidney`s face, and he thought that King was in an accident and that`s when the kidnappers took him. He was sure of it. The accident was to incapacitate him to make it easy to take him. He still wasn`t sure if the accident was part of the kidnap. I must find King before it`s too late, he was overwhelmed. "You know, accidents like that happen all the time," he said. "Even to famous people."

"I know, I hope he`ll be all right and nothing happens to his imagination," William said sadly.

"That`s why we all have to very careful always, " Sidney said sternly."You know, Will, I don`t think you understand what`s going on." Sidney decided to tell William everything.

"What do you mean?" William felt uneasy.

"You see Will, Stephen King has been kidnapped. I don`t know by whom or why,"

Sidney`s voice was solemn but steady. "I think there`s something strange about his accident. I`ve been getting visions and having suspicions as to where he is held captive and I`m certain he`s not in Maine. I`ve spent some time there, where he was born, lived, but of course, whoever is responsible for his accident and kidnap wouldn`t be so stupid as keep him prisoner in Maine or even America. Would you like to come with me and help to free him?"

"Of course, I`ll come with you," William was bewildered. "Where shall we search. "I`m with you. "It`s a fascinating thing happening to you, Sid."

They weren`t drinking anymore, they hadn`t finished their beer

"I`m sure the F.B.I in America is on the case," William said thoughtfully.

"I don`t think the F.B.I or Interpol can handle what`s going on," Sidney said, his voice faraway.

William was completely baffled.

The weather changed: it became dark and foreboding and thunder rumbled.

Sidney hurried off with William following.

Rain drizzled, it became darker almost black. Sidney didn`t mind getting wet, but everything bothered William.

"Will, I`ll understand if you don`t want to come with me," Sidney`s tone was of deep concern. "In this world, there are many people who are jealous of rich and famous people and would do anything to bring an end to them or kidnap them for ransom."

"I`m well aware of that, my dead friend," William seemed to feel his friend`s anguish and determination.

The rain was heavy now. William`s face was dripping. Sidney was soaked he didn`t mind.

8

Deep, deep underground, lit by torches, a man was strapped to an iron-chair, his face bruised, battered and bloody, but his eyes emitted a strange golden light.

A tall figure dressed in black, circled the captive on the iron-chair. The tall figure snarled, eyes red and flaming teeth animal-like, lips red.

"I read your MISERY novel all the time!" the tall figure was clad in snake-skin from feet to around the neck and barefooted, hair sandy and wild. "And I`ve found a way, a key to open a door to get to you! I`m evil! The Devil never had it so good! All those millions of books you`ve sold all over the world are making lots of money for you. I want some of it! You are rich! I am a frustrated critic who has been writing novels with the same themes as you and all I`m getting are rejection-slips. So now I`ve given up novel-writing and taken up criticism for a distinguished literary Supplement, read all over the world. Deep in my soul I still want to write a best-seller! I don`t want any money for your release. All I want is for you to write me in your stories where I triumph and outside the stories I`ll be able to find a publisher and become like you!" spit, blood and fire came from the tall figure`s snarling mouth. "If you don`t, I`ll kill you, or better still, make you a mad, crazy writer whom nobody wants to read anymore." Now laughter proceeded from the snarling red mouth.

"No one can find us, because we`re deep down in the bowels of earth. I can be were-wolf, vampire, any monster created by you. You couldn`t hide behind Bachman!"

Thunder boomed! The underground scene shook! Howls and snarls were heard all around. Then everything went black and disappeared.

9

There was a great flash of lightning. Then like sun and moon came together like a great eye in the heavens. Sidney and William were in America. William was dazzled as they floated through air but he wasn`t frightened. They were in Central Park.

Suddenly, a young woman came running towards them: it was Stephanie, they recognised her at once.

It was mid June.

They hugged each other happily.

"You`re here as well!" William said, surprised and almost losing his balance. "How did she find us?" His head swan with questions.

Sidney smiled broadly at both of them.

"Bill, there you are!" she sang to William. "How nice to see you!" as if she felt that William wasn`t pleased at seeing her.

She kissed both men.

The Park accommodated many people enjoying the summer sunshine. Trees and buildings seemed to sparkle.

William blinked and forced a wide smile.

They then went to a hotel off Fifth Avenue. The room was large and spacious. Stephanie was certainly doing very well in America, they thought.

The hotel was several stories high. The large room was on the seventh floor. A wide window was opened, light purple drapes drawn showed a bright, cloudless summer sky and a magnificent view of the city.

"We are in America, I gathered that much," William said, looking out of one of the two Windows. "It`s very nice. I`ve never been. Always meant to come here, but was always putting it off." He breathed deeply as if to take it all in one breath.

"Yes, baby, this is the Big Apple," Sidney joked. "We`re in New York, Manhattan.

"Where`s Stephanie?" William asked, turning to face Sidney.

"Oh, she went to the bathroom," Sidney replied from a comfortable arm-chair in a corner.

"But....but... I...I...I thought.... she... didn`t....I can`t understand....." William was confused, his face was reddish.

"I was only washing my face," Stephanie entered in her flowery cotton dress. "My face felt so sweaty. I also felt like having a shower."

Did she overheard us, William thought, now sitting in a sofa facing Sidney and looking at him intently.

Sidney returned William`s look, and they understood each other.

"I wonder who took him?" William changed the subject, now with a sullen look.

"Yes, I know about Stephen King's kidnap," Stephanie said thoughfully. "I've been keeping track of Sidney's whereabouts. "No one knows where they've holding him prisoner.

Wherever King is, he must know that his readers are extremely sad and angry and searching for him."

William stared at her in wonderment. Sidney was content with her.

"I know it's not like that zealous fan in the novel, MISERY," Sidney was in deep thought.

"That's too obvious. I believe it is simply a case of jealous gone mad."

William's stomach turned, "Some people are crazy."

"Everybody wants to be famous," Sidney said roughly. "We live in the celebrity culture.

That's why some people go to any extreme to be the public's eye, even committing the most heinous crime to be there."

Stephanie winced, "You can say that again, Of course, Sid, we aren't like these criminals."

They went searching discreetly around Manhattan until night. Stephanie offered them an adjoining room with a large bed and Sidney and William fell asleep in their jeans and shirts instantly because they were very tired.

10

There was a loud knock on the hotel-room door. Sidney turned, opened his eyes, yawned. The others were sound asleep. It was morning, the sun was streaming through window where they had forgotten to close the curtain-drapes.

Sidney got up slowly and quietly so as not to disturb William, opened the bedroom door, then slowly went to the hotel front door, opened it, yawned and sleepily looked at a medium-sized, distinguished-looking man in his late fifties, standing there, dressed in a grey tweed suit, black shining shoes. His face was familiar to Sidney.

"My name is Reavis, I`m a professor," the man said calmly, his light-blue eyes sparkling. He was greying at the temples but his face had a youthful look. He spoke with authority. "I`ve heard a lot about you from colleagues. I`ve come to meet you. I was educated at the Perse School in Cambridge, England and educated at Cambridge university. I`ve taught there for many years. I`ve written books on creative literature and I`m respected as a foremost 20th century crictic."

Sidney was completely taken aback. "Of course, yes, I`ve heard of you. Some people call you the eagle-eyed critic, not me, I respect most of your work. Yes, come in."

And Reavis followed him into the sittingroom. Reavis was shown and accepted a seat in an arm-chair. He looked around the sittingroom, then at Sidney who was facing him.

"Yes, it`s an honour to meet you," Sidney held out his hand again and they shook hands," he was over excited that such a well-respected man of letters came to see him.

"I hope I haven`t disturbed your slumber," Reavis surveyed the young man`s demeanour. He was extremely polite.

"Oh, no, I`m fully awake, you`re welcome," Sidney was now ready and refreshed.

William and Stephanie were now awake, their faces brightly welcoming as they came into the sittingroom, William in his crumpled white shirt and jeans and Stephanie in a blue cotton dressing-gown.

Sidney introduced them to Reavis and they sat looking at each other.

"I know we`re here for one purpose," Sidney announced with confidence. "We were brought together for a quest to find the author Stephen King."

They looked at him, agreeably nodding their heads.

"What we`re going to encounter !" he didn`t mean to raise his tone. "We`ll need the strongest will and fortitude. Because if we don`t, we are going to fail, and Stephen King as we know him will cease to exist."

The morning sunlight suddenly filled the room, outside, birds sang merrily.

"We`re going to see and do wonders, my friends," Sidney was jubilant as the sunlight spotlighted his face.

The surroundings disappeared, and Sidney, William, Stephanie and Reavis were on top of a mountain; a cooling breeze was sweeping over them, refreshing their senses, the sky was at its bluest.

They were still in America, but where, they didn`t know at the present time.

Professor Reavis began to feel the cool air penetrating his entire being, he relaxed with utter joy and contentment, "This King is a King of writers," he muttered.

"We`re somewhere in wild west, I think!" William looked around at vast terrain all around.

"No! No! Do not say where we," Sidney warned. "We don`t know who is listening and tracking us. We must only guess. Keep our location to ourselves. These kidnappers are very clever. For now, we are somewhere in America, that` all we need to say."

"Right," William nodded.

Stephanie and Reavis said together, "We understand."

"How could he have been kidnapped without anyone seeing or suspecting anything?" speculated sorrowfully.

"I`ve told you before, William, the kidnappers have been planning this for a very long time. They`re using all sorts of state-of-the-art equipment. And, also, I believe they have a brilliant clairvoyant. That is why I stress, we must keep quiet about our whereabouts."

They saw birds, vultures, butterflies, cactus, tumbleweed, grasshoppers, rattle-snakes, rabbits; heard the sounds of wailing cayotes, the growls of mountain-lions. They encountered valleys, wide rivers and sometimes leafless trees, giant rocks and human tracks. On and on they journeyed in America, North and South, East and West, meeting and talking to the native peoples and strangers: asking tactful questions, always secretive and careful. in summertime, Spring, autumn and winter. They were well-equiped with money and other necessities. They stayed in hotels, motels and boarding-houses.

"What now, sweet Prince," said Reavis to Sidney one Saturday just before noon in Miami as they were leaving their hotel. Reavis` tone showed worry.

"Well, I think all the clues and signposts are to be found in King`s stories," Sidney replied thoughtfully.

"Yes, yes," replied William and Stephanie together.

"I see, I read all of them," said Reavis matter-of-factly. "The Miami air will certainly invigorate us." And he looked skyward.

They were all dressed in jeans, sleeve-less shirts and plimsolls. Reavis wore a panama-hat.

"It`s a beautiful country," William said, looking around.

Stephanie was all smiles. Reavis was always deep in thought.

Sidney suddenly saw deep in his consciousness, a vision of a native American, an Apache in native dress, beckoning him on. Sidney remained quiet for a long while as the others chattered. He was in deep meditation as the Apache spoke to him in his mind, a kind of native telepathy or thought transference: "I am Gnik. I`ve come to be with you on your journey in this land. Keep faith." And the voice faded away. Sidney was sitting on a little hill over a canyon.

The others were searching around, but they could take in the vast panorama all at once.

"He`s obviously not here," William uttered tiredly.

"Are you tired, my boy?" Reavis asked him somewhat cheerfully.

"I`m not, it`s rather very interesting," said Stephanie gaily.

"Let`s have some refreshments, then," Sidney said, coming out of his meditation with a pleasing smile.

They say on a grassy plain and ate sandwiches, drank coffee, tea and chocolate.

"I think King is being held prisoner somewhere deep underground," Sidney said, sipping a glass of white wine. "I`ve had this feeling all along."

"That could be anywhere," William remarked, chewing slowly.

"We must keep our hopes up always," Reavis said reassuringly, also sipping white wine.

"I don`t think it`s in America," put Stephanie, sipping a glass of water.

"Mr. Prince will get the directions," said Reavis, "he has a special gift."

"I`m getting bits at the present time," said Sidney, looking at each of them. "It`s not very clear. I have to connect the dots and make sense of the bits and pieces. I`ll get there."

"Do you know exactly who has kidnapped him." asked an impatient William.

"Whoever has him, isn`t going to kill him," Sidney was solemn. "I think, they`ve injected some kind of drug which makes him not himself. That`s why we must be very careful. I must stress this over and over again."

Their spirits were lifted as they felt Sidney`s words reaching into their hearts. Then they moved on.

They were now on an aeroplane, flying from Miami: they were the only passengers on the aircraft. They sat close together.

"The kidnappers of King are using a very powerful invisible barrier which is very difficult to penetrate without the correct clues," Sidney announced. "I think I might be able to summon Shakespeare as a guide."

"What!" the others exclaimed together, staring at each other.

"You can do that, Sid,?" William said in utter amazement.

"I`m sure he can," Reavis smiled. "That`s why I`m with him."

"This is going to be a wonderful adventure," Stephanie beamed. "I intend to enjoy every moment of it."

"O, brave new world with such creatures in it," Reavis paraphrased and felt a satisfaction in the depths of his soul.

They now believed that they were entering a new world or another dimension.

"Remember, anything is possible in the world of Stephen King said Reavis brightly. "One must know how to read and understand his stories." Then he held out his hands to them, they touched them, and Sidney said Stephen King`s name three times.

And to their utter astonishment of his three companions, a man who looked and dressed like William Shakespeare appeared standing between and looking at each of them. They looked disbelievingly at the figure. Only Reavis seemed to be at ease.

William`s and Stephanie`s eyes almost popped out of their sockets. William was a little afraid, he felt he was in a dream or hallucinating. Stephanie calmed down then forced a little smile.

"Dear readers and spectators, I am William Shakespeare!" the figure announced in a Warwickshire accent. "Sometimes called the Bard. Believe I am he. With this fellow King I have managed to come to you, not as a ghost but in the reality of living flesh and blood. I shall be your companion on this quest."

They all felt an overpowering sensation taking over their entire bodies. William was a little afraid. Stephanie trembled. But Reavis` joy was beyond reason, he felt he was a new man. And Sidney was smiling all over.

"What a piece of work is man!" Shakespeare recited. "What a piece of work is Stephen King! Oh, I am excited at the way words are used in the twenty-first century. I turn in my grave at American wit. Don`t be afeard of me gentle people ."

"Beloved Bard, I think you should dress in the manner of the twenty-first century," Sidney smiled at Shakespeare. "We don`t want to attract attention."

"Yes, of course, sweet Prince," Shakespeare answered cheerfully. "Only you and your companions are able to see me."

"The Maestro is with us, God be praised," said Reavis, his face shining with glee and a spark ran through his body and his being throbbed with renewal.

Sidney was carried away with excitement and as he took a hand of Shakespeare and kissed it and said respectfully, "Welcome to our company, great Bard!"

His companions chanted the same welcome, their faces smiling. William and Stephanie were now at ease.

Shakespeare smiled at them, "Thank you, kind friends! I hope I shall be of great service to you. An artist can never please everybody. To try would be a disaster." And turning to Reavis, he said, "I have seen your writings about my plays and poetry. You are a very interesting critic. I appreciate most of the things you have written. But there is one, maybe two things I do not agree with. But that is the way of your world and my world. The way of human kind and their scholarship. But all of that is for another time."

"Well put, Maestro," Reavis was all aglow.

"I have a pair of trousers long-sleeved brown shirt and a tweed jacket and a pair of patent leather shoes and brown felt hat," Sidney was producing these items from a large black bag he carried. " They are all your size."

"Oh, indeed I do, yes, thank you, sweet Prince," and Shakespeare went behind a nearby wall and changed into twenty-first century clothes. "Everything fits!" he exclaimed, coming to face them. "How do I look. You are my mirror!"

"You look fine," Sidney was happy.

"You would look good in any gentleman`s wear," Reavis beamed.

"A man from the Elizabethan age in modern dress, who would believe it," said Stephanie jokingly.

"It looks all right, yes," William said, walking around Shakespeare and surveying the fit. "You certainly chose the right tailors, Sid."

"Come on, let us be on our quest!" Shakespeare called, walking off but seeming to float off the ground. "This King fellow is like the holy grail of the twentieth century."

"Yes, let`s carry on!" Sidney chanted, following the Bard with the others behind. Looking back at them, he said, "Now we`re in another dimension!"

An ecstasy sweetened their bodies and they were carried away on the crest of a great cool breeze. Rock-and-Roll music were heard from afar. They went through New England, and the Bard wondered why it was called New England. "Isn`t it strange, mankind seeks, settled and creates a new life but still there is a hankering for the past home. That breeds uncertainty and can lead to chaos."

The weather was hot and brilliantly sunny. Breezes sang in trees. They saluted mighty majestic redwood trees. Their senses were charged with new senses of a different reality.

Without speaking, Sidney began to send thought-waves all around: "STEPHEN! STEPHEN! Where are YOU?"

Shakespeare waved his hand and said, "Here we are, my companions," and a grassy plain appeared with a picnic-spread of roasted chicken, slices of ham and beef, wine, bottles of beer and juices, grapes, loaves of bread, knives, forks, spoons, glasses, cups, plates and napkins.

They rested, sitting on the grassy plain and enjoyed the refreshments. Only Stephanie wasn`t eating, she sipped water only.

"Don`t you ever get hungry?" William asked, his face distraught.

"I`m all right, don`t worry about me," Stephanie replied simply, with a faraway look. "I`ll get by."

"Man shall not live by bread alone!" Shakespeare intoned, between sips of red wine and smacking his lips, said, "And I suppose women also shall not live by bread alone."

"Well put, great Bard," said Reavis, also sipping wine.

"She`s fine, she`s all right," Sidney smiled, drinking apple-juice.

But William remained puzzled, chewing his ham-sandwich slowly.

"You will understand that I cannot join in the food, only a little wine for me," Shakespeare said calmly. "But I will enjoy watching you eat to your satisfaction!"

Reavis burped loudly and smiled contentedly.

William chuckled and spilt a little of his salad, licked his lips and had another helping.

Shakespeare put his arms around William`s shoulder and calmly said, "Young Sir, you who carries my first name. The honey of the wine will soothe and open up your senses and bring leaps in body and spirit which will enable you to understand many mysterious things."

11

The tall, dark figure, deep, deep underground, snarled, teeth flashing, circled around the captive strapped on the iron chair, said angrily, "Aha! I see the young Prince fellow is on your trail! He`s very clever, very resourceful! But he`ll fail. Because my barrier is strong enough to keep him away!" And then he laughed and laughed from the depths of soulless being and the laughter filled the whole underground area. "In your imagination, write me as a hero of goodness and light! Make me the good one! I`ll know what you`re thinking. You can`t hide your creative thoughts from me! When you write me in your creative imagination as all goodness, then I`ll release you! And then you wouldn`t be able to change me back to my evil self! Do this, and I`ll give you more than the Nobel Prize!"

The captive in chains on the iron chair, screwed up his face, surprisingly smiled and spat blood at his captor.

"Fuck you, then! Suffer, if that`s your sacrifice!" The tall, dark figure bellowed, farted, punched, kicked and head-butted his captive. "You damn fool! Critics laugh at you! Call your work pulp fiction nonsense and pop rubbish. They call you a horror writer, meaning you`re a horrible writer. They never put you in the category of, Tolstoy, Dickens, Henry James, Melville, Mark Twain, George Eliot, Conrad, Jane Austen and the Brontes`! Why! Why haven`t they done that? Ask yourself why? Get away from all that and write me into something they would accept and I`ll most likely win the Nobel Prize! I can never write like you. I don`t want to anymore!"

Thunder boomed again! Screams, shouts, snarls were heard all around!

"You`re King in name only! Ha! Ha! Ha! Ha!" the tall, dark figure mocked. "The literary establishment ignores you. They are bursting with jealousy of your mass audience!"

12

When Sidney, his companions and Shakespeare had finished their meal, Shakespeare held up his hands and said, "All it takes is, humility and faith in one's self!" And with these words the remainder of the food and the picnic-spread disappeared. "Now we must be on our way.

The King has little time left! I have been thinking, your modern world has some wonderful things, but also some terrible things. The wonderful things are wasting away in your modern world. Few critics have understood what I was doing in my plays and sonnets. This modern world of yours has too much hubris. Young Prince, your love and respect for Stephen King are all writers need and understanding and readership!" He smacked his lips and walked off.

"To be in this New World, brave and daring!" he thought and his being was all smiles.

They came to some steps leading steeply upwards surrounded by bush and trees. Shakespeare began to climb dexteriously. A mist began to encircle them, drifting upwards.

"Let us clear this bush and make it clear to ascend!" Shakespeare said and began clearing away bush and over-hanging vines.

Sidney and his friends sprang to the task, pushing away, breaking and cutting bush and over-hanging branches.

"I wonder where do they lead?" said Reavis, looking around and upwards.

Maybe heaven or some kind of remote paradise, thought Stephanie, clearing the steps.

"My dear, Professor," Shakespeare with a soothing voice, "we are on our way to find the the writer of immaculate fiction." Shakespeare showed no signs of tiredness.

"Just as you say, great Bard," Reavis smiled.

A path was cleared with mossy parts in the middle of the stone-steps, but the top of the steps couldn`t be seen.

Suddenly, it darkened Shakespeare looked around suspiciously. "Your modern climate might be changing unexpectedly." His voice was solemn. "I suppose that is the price you pay for technological progress." Then he laughed heartily. "Don`t mind me. I am admiring many things in your modern age. I wish I had them in my age, I probably would have written better plays."

Carefully, they made their way up the steep steps, clearing a pathway as they went.

Shakespeare floating upwards leading the way with Sidney behind and the others bringing up the rear.

Up and up and up they climbed as if on a ladder to the clouds.

Shakespeare stopped, turned and looked down at them.

Sidney wasn`t panting, the others were panting profusely, especially Reavis and William.

"Be strong! Keep the faith! The exhaustion will leave you!" Shakespeare announced, his voice echoing through the minds of Sidney and the others and throughout the area.

And the tiredness left them and they felt refreshed.

Sidney was enchanted.

They finally reached the top: it was flat like a plateau, grassy smooth, about the size of a soccer-pitch. From here they peered down in a huge valley with green trees and a few houses dotted around.

"From here we shall see many wonders!" Shakespeare said and waved his hands about.

"But, where are we?" William asked confused. "Are we in America?"

"We must never speak out where we are!" Sidney reminded them. "I`ve already told you that. We could be somewhere in Europe, England or, yes, America. Please, follow the Bard and I. We won`t lead you astray!"

"Well said, young Prince," Shakespeare said calmly.

"I`m with you all the time," said Reavis, well-pleased.

"I can feel many things!" said Sidney, looking around, surveying the scene.

"Use your heart and soul to see and feel everything!" instructed Shakespeare. "Be like your friend, Prince! He is using a higher form of consciousness."

Reavis took a deep breath and closed his eyes and visualised blue mountains, flowers, lawns, a green and a blue waterfall into a turquoise lake. He was dazzled and felt that he had left his body. He regained himself again and was fulfilled.

William felt a soft music of harps playing through his body and he felt he was both masculine and feminine at the same time, a sweet sensation coursed through his body.

Stephanie farted the sweetest perfume and urinated nectar.

Shakespeare and Sidney held hands and said together, "They have it. They are truely with us now!"

"The barrier shielding the prison where King is imprisoned is very strong," Sidney`s eyes were closed as he meditated deeply. "I can`t penetrate it, not yet."

They were walking around the plateau and then down into the valley.

"All I can see is, King is chained to an iron-chair," Sidney said sadly. "It`s like hell in that underground cell. The place is vast and dark. All his books and stories are down there, on shelves, book-stands and tables." Then he bowed, bent down and put an ear to the ground, then he rose as he saw a golden light shining on Shakespeare`s face and a halo around his head.

"Sweet Prince, you truly understand the nature of King`s work," Shakespeare beamed at Sidney. "I wish people read me the way you read King. I salute you!. With you it is never an academic nor intellectual exercise!"

Sidney stared at his three companions, and they too saw the radiance of the Bard`s face and understood what he said about Sidney's reading. They too had a vision of King in a prison somewhere underground.

"Jealousy sometimes take over and destroy people," muttered Reavis, his eyes red and watery.

"Sweet friends, let us keep on going!" Shakespeare chanted. "We must not waste time. Time is precious to me! Remember, every quest is fraught with dangers! As long as you have faith, everything will be all right!"

"We understand, great Bard!" Sidney and his friends said together.

A refreshing breeze soothed their faces, birds sang sweetly in trees.

Then a voice boomed and broke their enchanting interlude. "You'll never find King! You cannot defeat me! I'm impenetrable!" And laughter filled the air. "Do you think I'll be foolish enough to be in the United States!"

Suddenly, Sidney and his three friends began to feel like they were burning up. It was too hot even for mid August. It felt like they were on fire.

Shakespeare winked at Sidney who began to recite passages from King's books and stories. Then he shouted, Stephen King reigns forever! Release him, you unworthy critic!"

"You must take King seriously!" Stephanie screamed.

"Aha, young lady!" the voice raged. "I think you're something from one of King's stories! You're unfinished! You're a freak, if not of King, of some other writer who was fed up with you. You're the one who never goes to the toilet! What a tragedy! I thought every living thing that consumes food must release the waste! You`re probably rotting on the insides! One of these days, you`re going to burst like a balloon filled with shit! And the stench will be unbearable, even poisonous! Your friends better be careful!"

Shakespeare gently touched Stephanie`s arm, head and face, and said, "I would have gladly put you in one of my plays. And they all vanished from where they were.

"The evil critic is going to take on many disguises," Sidney said thoughtfully as they whisked through another dimension.

"We`re with you, Stephanie!" said William and Reavis together.

"So young and so true!" remarked Shakespeare.

"I know where we are going!" called Sidney cheerfully.

"Yes, he knows!" Shakespeare intoned.

"I see and follow with all my heart and soul," Reavis said.

Stephanie felt very happy with her life for the first time: she wasn`t deformed nor was she a freak.

Sidney went along humming merrily. Then he said, "We had to come to America to get the correct coordinates to pick up the scent of King."

Shakespeare was glittering. William embraced Stephanie and kissed her.

"Everything is clear now," uttered Reavis.

They were now in a grassy field interspersed with pine, oak, chestnut and poplar trees; birds greeted them with enchanting songs which filled their bodies, taking away all doubt and exhaustion.

They came to a high street. Shakespeare disappeared. Reavis looked around, trying to make out the place where they were.

"Oh, he`ll be back," Sidney chimed.

They walked along the high street in a dazzling July sunshine, Sidney and William felt hungry. Reavis had other things on his mind.

"Let`s get some more food," said Sidney. "We are running out of our food supply."

They went to a supermarket and bought more food.

"I`m truly enjoying this adventure," Stephanie said to Reavis as they waited outside the supermarket. "More than anything I`ve ever done in my life."

"You are quite an extraordinary person, I must say," Reavis smiled. "I`m so glad I had the privilege of meeting and befriending you."

Stephanie was glowing with appreciation.

Sidney and William came out, laughing happily with knap-sacks filled with food.

And they continued their quest. As they went on, Sidney closed his eyes for a moment, opened them again, and looked around and he could make out various characters from Stephen King`s novels and stories, smiling and nodding at him.

Reavis and the others saw them as well.

"Are they real?" Reavis asked, staring, undressing the characters with his eyes

"Yes, they are, professor," said Stephanie, pointing.

"Yes, I remember them," William was excited, waving at the characters.

"That's no disguise," Sidney was filled with joy. "It shows we're on the right track."

"Yes, we are!" Reavis and Stephanie said together.

Sidney said, "I think I'll say hello to them."

"Shall we join you?" asked Reavis excitedly.

"Oh, no, no, that won't be necessary," Sidney shook his head.

"All right, you know best," returned Reavis, looking around."It's fantastic, isn't it!"

Sidney, smiling, went to the characters, greeting and shaking their hands and embracing them. They in turn were happy returning his greetings and happiness.

Reavis was breathing heavily, feeling that he was taking part in an epic novel.

"We're in the spirit of everything," Stephanie was all radiance.

"We could be inside one of King's novels," William's voice sounded faraway.

Sidney's companions were enchanted by the way Sidney moved amongst the characters. They felt they were also with him, inside his mind, moving together as one.

"We were supposed to be here," Sidney said gladly as he introduced the characters to his friends. Two male characters were, John Coffey, the huge black man from the novel, The Green Mile, and Lisery, from Lisery's Story. Both characters shook hands and embraced Sidney's friends, smiling and bowing to them.

Reavis felt a thrill running through his body, touching his very soul.

William and Stephanie both felt they were having a most gratifying orgasm.

In the magic of a few minutes, it was night, then day again; then it was a hot summer, then it was autumn, then winter, then Spring. Then they were in Europe, in Germany, then London, then Italy, then Canada, then Brazil, then China, then Africa; moving around the world with the imagination of Stephen King. Then back again with the characters. "This is pure heaven!" Reavis swooned and bowed to the characters.

Coffey placed his large fingers on Reavis` head for about seven minutes. All eyes were on them.

Reavis felt an overwhelming freedom he had never known before or knew existed: a complete freedom of mind.

"Everything about us is creative, a source of everlasting energy," Reavis` face was shining like gold. "I see and feel the great sweep of narrative! Magical creatures leaping into forever existence!" It was as if he was in a hypnotic state, relaxing and beautifully sweet.

Sidney`s face was lit with satisfaction.

"God Save This King!" Reavis was in a higher state of consciousness.

Coffey and Lisey smiled at each other and said, "The Professor has attained total fulfilment. He no longer has the academic intuition."

The others smiled full contentment. "Everything is possible in the world of Stephen King."

Mobiles ran! Most were ignored.

Then John Coffey and Lisey disappeared!

Sidney`s mobile rang! He answered.

The voice at the other end sounded ancient but firm and confident, "It is me, William Shakespeare! I am using one of the modern contraptions at last, very interesting. Yes, young Prince, I think you and your friends should be on your way soon! I must say, this modern world is noisy."

"Yes, all right, we`ll be on our way. Thanking for calling." Sidney was elated.

"I was curious to see how these mechanical toys work," Shakespeare went on. "I am also doing some sight-seeing. The people in this modern world are always in a hurry."

The phone went silent, and Sidney beamed to his friends, "It was Shakespeare. He said we must be on our way. I`ve received all the secret coordinates and vibrations I need from the King`s characters." He smiled the biggest smile.

13

Deep underground, howls, grunts, snarls, teeth flashing: the tall, dark figure, eyes dazzling red, circled the captive strapped to the iron-chair and spat, "Your Prince has found some clues, but that wouldn`t help him! He`ll go around in tangles. Come on, Stephen, give me your success, and I`ll be famous with an international readership like you. I wouldn`t write the kind of stories you write. That`s all I ask!"

The captive, Stephen began surprisingly to laugh loudly; the laugher filled the underground scene. A mobile-phone rang! The tall, dark figure searched his person but couldn`t find it on him. King`s laughter continued.

From the mobile-phone, a voice, old and weary but distinct,said, "Cowards die many times before their deaths. The valiant never dies!"

"Where is that fucking voice coming from?" the tall, dark figure raged. "Oh, these blasted mobiles play the fool sometimes! Show your mother-fucking self!"

"You can`t capture an author`s imagination!" replied the mobile`s voice. "You know you can`t kill him! You depend on his imagination for your survival! Release him!"

"No! No! No! Not until he gives me the power of creativity and success!" the tall, dark figure blasted, spitting blood. "I am cut off from his creative power. I am free from his pen!"

The captive-King`s laughter ceased.

"I am everywhere!" the voice from the unseen mobile phone declared, "release him, I say!"

"Off with you! You tired old fart!" shrieked the tall, dark figure.

Rock and Roll music began to be heard on the mobile.

"You can`t trick me!" the tall, dark figure blasted and farted loudly.

The Rock and Roll music stopped, the weary old man`s voice came on again, "All the characters from all of King`s work have given clues as to your location!"

The tall, dark figure slapped King hard on his face and shouted, "Man, they haven`t even given you a Pulitzer Prize!"

"A writer doesn`t need prizes to be a truly great and accomplished artist!" the mobile-voice said mockingly. "Remember what Sartre said: `a writer should not allow himself to be turned into an institution`. A large Readership, that`s the genius!"

"Get away from here!" the tall, dark figure boomed. "I`ve enough of your literary crap!"

King began to laugh again, this time from the depths of his soul.

"You`re only a figment of your own imagination!" and laughingly the voice from the mobile phone disappeared.

14

Sidney, Reavis, Stephanie and William met Shakespeare in London`s Oxford Street.

"The noise is affecting your delicate ear, Maestro?" Reavis laughingly said to Shakespeare who was surveying the stores, shops, cafés, road-side vendors, vehicles and people. "I`ve been here for a lecture at the London University, and I still can`t come to terms with the incessant noise and hustle. That`s a city for you."

"My dear, Professor, in all my plays," Shakespeare responded, "I have learnt to adjust to many roles. Indeed, your modern way is noisy but fascinating."

They walked down a side street, Sidney was whistling a current popular song.

"I think we should concentrate our efforts on the underground network," Shakespeare was cool and contained.

"Yes, Sir, of course," Sidney agreed, his face illuminated by his happy feeling as he looked around piercingly.

"Maybe the underground railway can be a gateway to where we have to go," said the Bard. "But we must watch out for tricks."

They were swamped with people. It was lunch-time no a late April Friday. Sidney and Shakespeare leading the way to an underground station.

"Amazing! We are like tourists!" Shakespeare said, his eyes gleaming, "The mechanical gadjets seem to rise out of earth, reaching for the sky."

Sidney felt a deep well of emotion boiling inside him, a kind of radar guiding him to a location.

They came to an underground station, newly-renovated and brightly lit. Some people looked at them suspiciously. They didn`t mind, they kept going, and it seemed endless: down and down into a forever crab-hole, their heads in one direction, it was as if the underground was leading down to the very depths of London.

And then, all the people, trains, lights and underground paraphanalia disappeared! It was now semi-dark. Steps had disappeared. Sidney and Shakespeare felt that they were being watched, even followed.

Then Shakespeare stopped, looked around and said, "My dear, Prince, I think we seem to have come to some kind of dead end."

"Yes, I think so too," answered Sidney, looking about him.

Reavis, William and Stephanie looked at each other quizzically.

"I wonder where this underground leads to?" said Reavis, now looking upwards.

Sidney kept on going, they followed, and came to a wide tunnel with a canal with running water in the middle.

"I feel something, I tell you! It's here somewhere! Come on, let's go on!"

They looked at each other, shrugged and looked at Sidney and nodded.

"Do not worry, we will be all right!" Shakespeare assured them and lit up their faces with a smile from his creative heart.

"All clues point to the entrance of this underground," Sidney surveyed the scene while talking. "We must move on! Come along!"

They heard a rumble, then a splash!, then a great pouring: the canal was beginning to flood.

"It's flooding!" Reavis and Sidney and Shakespeare shouted together and spun around like windmills.

Then the sound of an engine, a roar which wasn't a train's!

They stared puzzlingly at each other.

"Hold on tightly to each other!" Shakespeare commanded. "Do not let go! We will be safe!"

They held on to each other, becoming like a ball of swaying humanity. A great wind surrounded them.

The roaring sound of the engine came closer and closer, until it sounded all around them, then it stopped! It appeared as a red car with lights outside and inside, flickering like a Christmas tree.

All hearts were racing, except Shakespeare's. And they still held on together tightly.

"I'm the Voice this red car. I can travel on the rails, on the road and in the sky, floating like a helicopter" a voice from the red car blared out. "You are listening to a computer-brain in the vehicle and in your heads!"

Sidney realised that this car was like Blaine in the WILLOW AND GLASS section in the Dark Tower book. Shakespeare saw it too in Sidney`s mind and smiled.

"You are my cargo!" the voice of the car sang merrily.

"Why, of course, that`s it!" Reavis said and sensed and understood clearly what Sidney was transmitting.

Stephanie and William were also getting the vibrations.

"Let the air of creativity flow through your hearts!" Shakespeare`s voice chimed in their ears.

"Yes, yes, this car is taking us as cargo on our journey," Sidney explained. "The car has to go, CARGO."

The great wind had subsided.

Smiles of understanding on all faces and in hearts now as they entered the opening car doors of the talking car. The seats were soft and comfortable.

"Let`s be on our way!" the voice of the car, a computer-screen dash-board at the front seats, announced. "The car can go!"

And off they went, on the ground, above it and on the rails, soaring away like a gliding bird.

Faraway in the distance, they heard a grunt, a scream, then a sickly moan. But they were untroubled.

They came out into a forest which was unusually silent. The trees didn`t stir, they showed foliage, blossoms and others flowering. There wasn`t a wind nor breeze rustling through this forest. No birds, insects nor animals were visible. The car hovered about a foot from the ground which was grassy.

"This must be an enchanting forest of many fairy-tales!" Sidney said happily, looking around from the back seat of the car. His face dazzlingly bright, his eyes radiant.

They were filled with excitement and expectation.

Shakespeare soothed their hearts when he intoned, "A Midsummer`s Night Dream!"

The sky was cloudless and a sun lit up the still, silent forest.

They were always dressed for any weather, be it winter, summer, autumn or Spring, snowing, raining or dry season.

Stephanie clutched William`s arm tightly, they were also in the spacious back seat and William felt his heart dancing.

The car-doors opened! They got out.

"I`ve done my work!" said the car. "I shall be off now! By the way, my name is EIRRAC!

Best of luck!" And the car flew away like a bird.

"This must be another world of King`s imagination!" Sidney said thoughtfully.

"Yes, indeed, young Prince, Nature is my goddess, and yours as well." Shakespeare said.

"We`re on the right track," said William, his heart beating fast.

They heard voices, human ones, coming towards them.

Sidney and Shakespeare looked in the direction from where the voices were coming from.

The voices came nearer and nearer, until they were all around Sidney, Shakespeare and the others. They saw no physical bodies, only the sounds were pronounced.

"What, invisible people!" exclaimed William, looking around.

"Speak to us in a language that is intelligent!" Shakespeare called to the voices. "We can understand!"

One voice answered, the rest became silent as the forest. "I speak for everyone!" the voice said with authority. "Welcome to our world! What do you want?"

All this is like Dante`s journey in the Divine Comedy, Reavis thought and said, "Why have you no bodies? Are you ghosts?"

"Human bodies are so frail and weak!" replied the voice. "We prefer to be without them. I ask again, what are you doing here?"

"What is this place?" Sidney said, looking around. "Everything is silent here, why?"

"Please answer our question first!" the voice demanded. "Don`t answer a question with a question!"

"We are seeking a kind of holy grail!" Shakespeare said whimsically. Then laughed heartily.

"A holy grail! What is that?" the voice flew around Sidney and his companions.

"Our writer, Stephen King, has been kidnapped and held captive somewhere underground, and we want to rescue!" Sidney`s voice was shrill. "We have given up careers and livelihoods to do so!"

"Oh, now we see and understand!" the voice said in a compassionate tone.

"Please, help us!" Reavis, Stephanie and William said together.

"I`m not just a number one fan of King," Sidney`s voice was pleading. "It`s more, much more than that. When I read King`s work, I enter the stories and become part of them. And afterwards, I can do magical things!"

"That is extremely rewarding for you, young man!" the voice sang. "Now that you have answered our question. We`ll tell you who we are. But you must be prepared to withstand it. You have to be very strong. Everyone of you, except, the Bard!"

Sidney knew the exception meant Shakespeare whom he felt was impregnable. He was concerned about Reavis, Stephanie and William. He looked at them, his eyes radiating charm.

"Are you going to be able to take the revelation?" the voice asked.

"We too, will be able to take it!" Stephanie and William said together, their voices blending together like musical notes.

Reavis said bravely, "Of course, I can handle it."

"There are more extraordinary things on earth than are dreamt of in any philosophy!" Shakespeare chimed through their minds. "The imagination keeps us in touch with the divine."

"We are all ready!" they all said.

The sun came down and kissed their faces and there was fire in their eyes.

"I`d like to stay here, if I may!" Reavis was smiling and seemed to be under a kind of spell, an enchanting spell. "I`d like take off this academic cloak and enter the realm of pure creative thought!"

"That can be arranged, yes!" the voice replied.

Sidney, Stephanie and William looked at Reavis in amazement.

Reavis was elated.

"Now we are in the imagination of Stephen King!" the voice boomed. The silent forest was filled with the sounds.

They all began to float into the air about five feet above the ground. Stephanie and William hugged each other.

Shakespeare`s face was luminous with colours.

Then Shakespeare`s luminosity was streaming through the others, lifting their bodies and minds to a realm of creative energy beyond their wildest dreams. Shakespeare was in ripples of golden rays of light, chiming, expanding their thought-waves, then slowly all that was the Bard, disappeared.

Sidney and his companions were still floating above ground.

"Where? What has happened to Shakespeare?" William looked around quickly.

"He has done his work," answered Sidney happily. "He has returned to the divine heaven of all artists. Everything is going to be all right." Sidney`s head was held high and proud.

Stephanie and William kissed each other.

"We are characters who can only be born when the King decides!" the voice continued.

"Do you know where Stephen King is held captive?" asked Sidney with a loud, strong voice.

Ignoring the question, the voice said, "We can take on any form. Would you like to see what we can do?" the voice was playful.

"Now, who is answering a question with a question!" Sidney said reproachfully but gentle. "But it`s all right. We`d like to see what you can do."

"Well, young searchers!" chanted the voice. "Here we are!

And appearing before Sidney and his companions, in the wonderment of their minds, the voices materialised into heads without bodies, bodies without heads, bodies covered with eyes, bodies covered with mouths, a tall leg with an eye at the top and another at the bottom. Then they all disappeared, and then appeared again as blue, black, pink, red, yellow, brown, vermillion, green, white, orange and polka-dotted bodies with limbs, then bodies with wings and feathers flying around, eyes and mouths without bodies, bodies dripping liquid gold. "We are the characters yet to be created by the King. He might change us into something completely different. One day the reading world will wake up to our reality. Long live the King! He`s worth more than a Nobel Prize! Write on, Stephen!"

Then all the character-shapes disappeared. A man appeared walking along the ground, limping, his faced covered with a red plastic mask. "The pain has passed but I can still feel the pain of that accident!" he said, groaning with his masked head bowed.

Sidney`s face glowed as he was lowered to the ground, his arms outstretched to the man.

Stephanie and William were also on the ground now.

Reavis rejoined them after wandering around the forest.

The sky suddenly darkened into a flaming purple. Winds began to blow and howl. Now the trees, insects and other animals began to appear, making great noises! Then the limping masked man disappeared, and an old woman with flaming red eyes, flowing grey hair, dressed in black and brown rags, appeared and croaked, "I`m the Witch of Pages! I`m going to move mountains, kings and warriors! I`m going to hunt them down and correct the stories!" she laughed with a toothless mouth.

"Where is Stephen King?" Sidney called out bravely, standing erect, hands on hips.

"Don`t be so impatient, young Prince, Sir!" the Witch croaked. "We`re giving it to you slowly. You wouldn`t be able to take all of it in one go. It`s like a riddle!" Then she disappeared, and the limping masked man reappeared, a young woman`s face was haloed above him, calling out sweetly, "You`re on the right track! But there are immense troubles ahead!"

"I know. I`m ready for them!" Sidney felt stronger than ever.

"King is help captive somewhere in London!" the young woman`s voice was familiar. "You must use your penetrating wisdom to find the underground location. Deep into King`s works there are many clues!"

Sidney breathed deeply then looked pleasingly at his companions.

The haloed face of the young woman shone dazzlingly bright, lighting the whole area.

"Mr Prince, out of one story comes another!" the haloed young woman`s voice went on. "You must remember that you`re not only on a quest to find King, but you`re also being tested to see how truly and deeply you love and understand King`s work. You have to prove that you`re not one of those fans in love with King`s fame!"

Sidney reached into the deep recesses of his brain and said, "I`ve journeyed into the soul of King`s stories. I know what I`m doing with all my heart, soul and consciousness. King`s genius stirs the very fibre of my life"

"Imagine all the jealous people in the literary world coming together into one person of total jealous rage! That kind of jealousy creates a monster, more powerful than the green-eyed one!" the haloed young woman`s face kept changing into different colours as she spoke.

"That is the Thing that is holding Stephen King captive. The jealous- monster -Thing is very powerful and destructive!"

And to the mind-blowing wonder of Sidney and his companions, the haloed young woman`s face changed into Stephen King`s.

"Are you all right!" Sidney asked the Stephen King-image.

The face of King was tormented and battered but managed a little smile.

"Where are you exactly?" Sidney asked frantically. "It`s great to see you!"

Reavis, Stephanie and William stared smilingly at King`s face.

"Give us a sign, please, can you?" Sidney shouted, his face sweating.

The Stephen King face-image winked, nodded, then closed one eye, then changed back into the haloed young woman`s face.

"Wait! Come back! Tell us where! Who! What!" Sidney kept shouting.

"Calm yourself, young Prince," the haloed young woman`s face said soothingly. "Don`t get carried away yet!"

Sidney sighed heavily, collected his thoughts, then relaxed.

"Your friend, the Professor wants to stay here," the haloed young woman`s face said gently. And to Reavis, "Come to me, Sir!"

Reavis was shining with glee, his eyes popping, looked at Sidney and the others, then he rose off the ground and floated to the haloed young woman`s face, disappearing into it.

"Don`t worry about the Professor, he`s going to be all right!" the haloed young woman`s face went on."Your friend, Reavis is going to experience things beyond his academic imagination."

Stephanie and William felt a great throb in their chests.

Sidney sighed and a thrill like an orgasm soothed his whole being.

"I shall be with you always!" the haloed young woman`s voice was merry.

"We`ll never forget Professor Reavis," Stephanie and William said in unison.

"Reavis was a faithful companion, a true believer," said Sidney, "I shall carry him in my memory always. He`s with us in spirit. Now, I think, Stephanie, you and William should return to your homes. There`s something I have to see on my own. I will see you when I come back. Wherever you are, I`ll find you."

"I want to go on, I`m different as you know," Stephanie pleaded, she couldn`t understand this sudden decision. She looked around wildly.

"But....but I.....I...I..but....."William stuttered, "why... why..I...."

"It`s all right. I love you," Sidney`s voice was solemn. "Take care of yourselves." He hugged and kissed them. "Until we meet again."

Stephanie and William felt sad.

"We`re sorry we can`t come with you on the rest of the journey," said William, his voice breaking up a little. "But I understand now, yes. Take care of yourself."

"Yes, I understand as well, take care," Stephanie put on a smiling composure.

Then Stephanie and William stood away from Sidney, and a great beam spotlighted both of them, the spotlight circled them, brighter and brighter, until they were taken skyward from where the great beam was emanating; they managed a wave to Sidney who stood erect, looking up at them.

Sidney was now alone, looking again at the haloed young woman`s face, his face sad.

"Don`t be sad, young Prince!" said the haloed young woman`s face. "Now we`re on our way. Open up your imagination to the fullest. We are now travelling beyond your everyday world, beyond everyday time!"

And Sidney was whisked off in a flash, up in the now bright, blue sky cloudless with two suns.

15

Sidney was inside the haloed young woman`s face.

"Where is the Bard?" he asked, his eyes emitting a fiery glow, his face more youthful than ever.

"Shakespeare is only going to assist you if you are ever in dangers you can`t handle", replied the haloed young woman`s face. Her voice was stern.

Sidney realised he was flying through the air, through dimensions, through time-zones, through the reality of life and death, the air was cool and satisfying when it came through the eyes of the haloed young woman`s face and caressed his face.

The haloed young woman`s face sang sweetly, and he heard it vibrating his whole body, the voice was penetrating his very soul.

"The most beautiful melody I`ve ever heard," he said softly and his voice trailed off into deep space.

"I`m glad you like it," the haloed young woman`s face sang. "Are you in need of your kind of nourishment?"

"I was a little hungry a while back, but now I feel completely fed. "Your system has given me all I need, thank you."

"We always provide. Did you enjoy it?"

"Very much Sidney smiled.

"Your former friends are well-fed as well. You still have a lot to learn on this journey."

Sidney felt sleepy, he yawned, stretched his arms and laid on a patch of soft velvet green grass and fell fast asleep, and the amazing thing of it, his heart stopped beating.

"Our young Prince is at rest," the haloed young woman's face said gently.

in his deep sleep, Sidney was travelling faster than the speed of light, and in his dreamland, he was in the audience as Stephen King was receiving the Nobel Prize. Shakespeare, J .K Rowling, Homer, Dickens, Tolstoy, Faulkner, Poe, Herman Melville, T.S.Eliot, were cheering and clapping enthusiastically. Another dream-scape, showed Sidney's book, entitled, STEPHEN KING AND THE WRITING OF FICTION, an international bestseller. In the dream-world, Sidney was muttering, "I don't ever want to wake up. Don't wake me up. Let me live in this dream ."

"He's having the dreams of his life," the haloed young woman's face said sweetly. "All dreams can come true if you believe in them with all your heart and soul." The haloed young woman's face changed into a large computer-screen showing the words: WRITE THAT BOOK OF KING. WRITE IT IN THE CLEAREST LANGUAGE.

16

Stephanie and William found themselves in a strange land which could have been anywhere in Europe or North America. It was late summer. The sky was bright blue with a few little white clouds. Birds and bees sang and buzzed in the crisp early September air. The trees of birch, poplar yew, oak and willow were radiant green as they sway in a gentle breeze. Flowers delighted with their intoxicating perfume illuminating colours.

Stephanie gave a sigh of relief, a love and inspiring current ran through her body.

"We must be somewhere near where King is!" she called to William, her voice echoing around the summery scene.

William smiled and was uplifted by the assurance in her voice. "Where are we going?" his voice chimed through the trees.

"Stevey! Stevey! Where are you?" Stephanie was singing gaily, as she danced around, the bushes, behind trees, looking up into the trees, calling, calling King`s name. "King! King! Tell us where you are! Give us a sign, however small!"

William looked at her strangely.

"You are looking in the wrong place!" a bird-voice twittered in both their ears.

"Did you hear that!" they said together and looked at each other.

They came to a park and sat on a park-bench.

A ray of sun suddenly slanted through a nearby oak tree and spotlighted a man limping with a stick, his face glowing, coming towards them.

Stephanie and William stared starry-eyed at the stranger, nearer and nearer he came, his face glowing brighter as he drew nearer. They couldn`t recognise his face.

When he approached them, about a yard away, they still couldn`t make out who he was, the powerful glow hid his face; he held out a hand, waved and said, "You are truly brave readers and participants. But I`m afraid he`s not held captive anywhere here. He`s not held in the United States nor Canada. His captors would never risk. You already have sustenance from his home place. His captors are also working with a Shaman or magician.

"Do you know where King is held?" Stephanie said sternly, her lips pouting.

"Yes, but that would be too easy for you," the limping man replied, glowing brighter than before. "Remember, there`s no journey without hazards. Nothing worthwhile is easy. Hard work is the key to any existence. Great suffering brings great rewards. You have to solve all kinds of riddles. When you triumph, you will be worthy to be called true believers of King`s imagination."

"More riddles," William ventured, looking around and surveying the limping man closely. "I feel we are going around in circles."

"My friends!" the limping man`s voice was forceful, "I know where you came from! I know what you`re experiencing. Remember, as always, keep the faith. Now you will have a solid mind-set, tenacious character spirit, from all the stories of King. There are pathways in the imagination not ventured by the average reader. You must take those pathways."

Now the ray of sun spotlighted William and Stephanie together, brighter than before, they closed their eyes, took a deep breath. When they opened their eyes the limping man was gone.

Stephanie and William stared at each other completely overwhelmed.

"It`s really mind-boggling the way things happen when one reads King," said Stephanie.

"Yes," William sighed, "I don`t ever feel my former self anymore. I see the world in many colours. There are infinite possibilities."

Stephanie felt her soul rising out of her strange body. "We are getting it, Will, penetrating the true realities of fiction," she was ecstatic.

"And that limping man, is a riddle of when King had his accident, yes, "William said thoughtfully

"Dear William, we are journeying in the pages of Stephen King," Stephanie`s voice was singing.

"Where do we go from here?" William mused.

There were few people around.

"Follow our instincts, yes, you know," Stephanie said, smiling, put an arm around William`s waist and he did the same and they walked out of the park which was now filling with sunlight and more people.

17

In a wide, flat green field with flowers of every colour and description, Professor Reavis was walking around, his mind swimming with many questions. He laughed, jumped, sang, danced and whirled around. He was filled with every food and drink that are possible, like the nectar of the gods. He belched contentedly.

"This must be heaven, a heaven of fiction!" he sang loudly, his face red and shining. An echo in his ears answered: "Sing the King! On the road to the KING DOM!"

The pages of all of King`s books filled the air flying around like birds and butterflies. Reavis too, began to fly around like a happy bird. "Oh, I love them all!" he chanted. "I shall be a Professor of Stephen King!" He opened his mouth as wide as possible and all the words from all the flying pages flew into his mouth and swelled his whole body like a balloon and he alighted on the branch of an oak tree and resumed his former size.

"The possibilities are endless," he smiled all over, his mind fully opened, he entered King`s work as a baby, then a toddler, then a school-boy, then he was at university, then a lecturer, then a professor. He travelled from story to story, changing as he entered each one, and every experience heightened his brain, illuminated torches behind his eyes. He saw correct words for his innermost feelings. Then the sun, moon and stars began to dance in his brain. Animals played music instruments and sang melodies clear and true which caressed his soul. He sang with birds, though he had never heard the melodies before. It was music Bach and Mozart would`ve loved and composed. Then he was changed into a nightingale, then a sparrow, then a monkey, then a platypus, then back to himself.

A parrot with rainbow colours said, "Why hasn`t Stephen King won the Nobel Prize? Why? After all, he`s a master of creative fiction with an international readership! Fiction is a magical tale, something created out of nothing, showing the power of the human imagination! Power! Power! Brain —Power!"

Reavis turned inside out and outside in. He was something else in the wonder of King`s powerful imagination. Then he descended to the ground and began to dance, he danced and danced with a fire in his body he never knew he had.

18

In a field somewhere in England`s green and pleasant land, Reavis sat on the damp early morning grass as the dawn sun settled on his much-travelled face . It was mid-July.

"With all this time-travelling, I feel completely made-over", he muttered to himself. He was dressed in jeans, white short-sleeved shirt and brown- and- white sneakers. "H.G. Wells was right about time-travel. King makes it possible in our time." He tried to get up but his legs failed him. He heard merry singing coming towards him. He tried again to rise, with all his strength, and this time he rose, and saw coming out of a nearby green and flowery forest, men and women dressed like minstrels with flutes, lutes, drums and cymbals. Reavis rubbed his eyes and looked again, hard.

"They look like they came straight out of the Middle Ages," his voice trembled. "I wonder if this in one of Prince`s clever tricks. I can`t remember which story this is from."

The minstrels approached him, singing sweetly and dancing happily, they moved around him in a circle. Reavis stared at them searchingly. Then they stopped, and a tall, slim man with a smiling face, said to him, "Welcome, my friend to our land of amusement! Tell us, where are you from?"

Reavis looked at him from head to feet then at the others and anxiously answered, "I`m from twenty-first century earth. I`m a professor, well, I used to be a professor of English at a university in England. I`ve been on a journey of discovery, and this land seems to be a stop on my way."

The tall. slim man, dressed in green and purple costume of the Middle Ages, laughed heartily and said, "You are in the land of Roses. We are in full bloom, my friend. Here, music and merriment are all we live for."

"Don`t you cultivate the land? Build houses? What about technology?" Reavis` voice was surprisingly stern. "What about books, libraries?"

"All those questions!" the tall, slim man smiled. "And the answers are: we let those things take care of themselves. The books are written by a magician. We don`t know his name. Not yet anyway. The roses are our brothers and sisters, nature takes care of their every need. We never pick the roses. Roses are flowers of life. We eat fruits only. Our lives are spent in reading. Our magician-creator has a royal name. We are not allowed to say it in vain."

Reavis thought he had an answer to a riddle of where King was held, and said, "Yes, your creator has the name of a monarch, yes?"

"Yes, but it has to be the correct name, there are many," the tall, slim man was grave. "You must be very careful in choosing the right royal name. We live in an enchanted forest and we are satisfied and happy."

The other minstrels stopped their dancing and assembled themselves all around, reading.

"Which story is this?" Reavis was becoming impatient.

"A book of wonder which is still in the imagination, yet to be written and published. The tall, slim man leapt in the air, and descended slowly and said, "Let us take you to our leaders!" And he led Reavis with the other minstrels following, singing, jumping and dancing.

Reavis` head throbbed with music the gaiety, his heart beating fast and he sweated profusely.

The sun blazed, the sky was wide and clear and dazzlingly at its bluest. They came to a hill on top of which stood a castle with spires high in the sky. A cobbled pathway led to a huge wooden door which opened with a loud creaking sound. The minstrels followed the tall, slim man through, still singing and dancing happily.

Suddenly, they all fell silent as they entered a wide courtyard where a small crowd had gathered.

"THE KING!" a voice boomed above the crowd. "THE KING is coming! Long live THE KING!"

Reavis staggered into the courtyard, the crowd parted, making way for him as he came to the front. Looking upwards to a high balcony, Reavis saw a man dressed in twentieth-century clothes. Reavis was puzzled and he looked around for the tall, slim man but he was now standing next to the man dressed in twentieth-century clothes who was hailed as The King.

"Sire," the tall, slim man addressed the King, smiled and said, pointing to Reavis, "This man was found in your magical kingdom. I think he is searching for something. He is on a long journey. He means us no harm. He is a professor of language."

Reavis couldn't see the face of the man dressed in twentieth-century clothes clearly but he had a strange feeling taking over his entire being.

The King whispered in the tall, slim man's ear.

"Do you firmly believe in the Kingdom of the real creative imagination?" the tall, slim man shouted down at Reavis.

"Of course, of course!" Reavis shouted back. "I was with a young man named Sidney Prince, and somewhere along the way, I decided to come out of that journey and take another. Prince has shown and given me some remarkable insights! Yes, I'm a believer!"

And he looked around at smiling, happy faces and felt completely safe with them.

The KING whispered again in the tall, slim man's ear.

"All right!" the tall, slim man called down to Reavis. "You can come up and have an audience with the KING!"

Reavis quickly went up stairs, passing through spacious hallways, large beautifully decorated rooms and then onto the balcony where the KING stood with the tall, slim man. As Reavis approached, the face of the KING was completely blotted out. Reavis rubbed his eyes, then opened them again, rubbed again unbelievingly, opened them, straining but still couldn't make out the face nor personage of the

KING. Am I going blind, he thought, no, I can see all the other faces but not the KING`S.

"Welcome to our land," the KING greeted Reavis with a pleasant voice from the blotted out face, but the words seemed to come from the tall, slim man`s mouth.

"No one can see my face if they are not ready," again the words seemed to come from the mouth of the tall, slim man

"I`m ready, willing and able," Reavis stressed, his brow lined, his face hard and determined. "I believe in Stephen King`s work."

"What about those unfinished adventures?" the tall, slim man stood erect as the words came out of his mouth.

The crowd clapped and cheered!

"What unfinished adventures? I`ve never started anything I couldn`t finish," Reavis was impatient.

"An academic like you cannot be completely ready?" the tall, slim man said sternly. "Are you solidly sure you have wiped the slate clean?"

"I`ve been through all that transformation," Reavis seemed fed-up, a shadow passed over his face. "People can change their ideas. And with Stephen King, one`s view of the literary imagination can radically alter. I know that King isn`t dead. His illumination brightens our hearts."

"Then see the face of belief!" And to Reavis` utter astonishment, the face of Sidney Prince became visible and clearer on the blotted face of the KING –figure.

The minstrels, the crowd, the castle, disappeared! Reavis and Sidney were now standing in a green meadow with thick forest all around them.

"Where? How did you do that? What!" Reavis spun around like a windmill, his arms flapping like birds` wings, his eyes popping. "What a trick to play on an old friend, eh!"

"Well, I had to test you," Sidney smiled and said jokingly, his face taking on a brighter aspect. "I must say, you`ve passed with flying colours. You`re not an academic anymore."

"Actually," Reavis sat on the ground, then stretched out, lying on his back, looking up at Sidney and a blue sky, and said, "Some academics are quite engaging and fulfilling. For others it`s just a job."

Sidney had a strange look, "Changing the subject, professor, last night I heard a bellowing. I couldn`t make it out."

The sun flowed on them, wrapping them in hot but comfortable warmth.

"Maybe it was one of the hazards of the journey," Reavis` stomach rumbled. "I`m hungry and I`m out of food."

"Don`t worry, I have sandwiches and bottled water in my knapsack," said Sidney gaily.

"Thanks very much, you certainly think of everything."

Sidney`s knapsack contained, sandwiches, bottled water and other drinks, apples, bananas a cake and sweet biscuits.

Reavis ate to his heart content and belched, satisfied.

"Aren`t you having any?" he asked, licking his lips. "You don`t ever seem to eat or get hungry?" Reavis was gulping. "You`re an extraordinary phenomenon."

Winds rustled the trees and sounds which came were like a chant in agreement: "Yes, Sir!

Yes, Sir!"

"I`ve had my nourishment," Sidney said, looking around.

"And I can guess what that was," Reavis chewed slowly.

Suddenly, three black birds flew out of the forest and began to circle them.

"Birds always know when food is being eaten," Reavis threw some bits of the sandwich to the birds who didn`t go after the food, but looked strangely at the two men.

More birds began to fly out of the forest, flocks of them surrounded the two men.

"Get up!" Sidney ordered Reavis, "we have to get away from here quickly!"

"But I don`t understand, the birds were only attracted by the food," Reavis rose reluctantly, his mouth full and chewing.

Now there were thousands of black birds surrounding them, blackening the sky: they cawed, pecked, squawked and darkened the forest.

Reavis kept throwing food at the birds who showed no interest in the food.

Sidney began to hurry towards the forest with Reavis stumbling along behind.

"I can`t understand," Reavis blurted out, "why are you heading towards the forest which is filling with the creatures? Shouldn`t we be heading towards a town or built-up area?"

"Believe me, I know what I`m doing," Sidney said reassuringly. "In a thickly-wooded area we have a better chance than an exposed area leading to a town or city. I`m going into the deepest part of this forest," Sidney wasn`t even breathless.

Reavis picked up a stick and waved it at the birds, some scattered but didn`t go away.

Far off, they heard a roar like thunder, the sky darkened and all the birds began to disappear.

Reavis burped and farted. Sidney smiled.

"That sounds like a storm coming!" Reavis shouted. "We`re going to get caught in it."

"I don`t think it`s a storm," Sidney said moving along quickly. "Let`s go deeper into the forest."

As they went deeper and deeper into the forest, trees and bushes began breaking down, uprooting, and a rough pathway with a giant computer appeared in front of them. The broken branches and bushes began to shake as if a giant hand was shaking them.

"Write it so that all may read! Who is going to right/ write it?"

Reavis farted loudly and grabbed hold of Sidney`s arm.

"I`m not the writer!" Sidney answered bravely. "I`m searching for a master writer who was kidnapped. He`s the inspiration of my reading life. Do you know where he`s held?"

"Yes, but I`m not going to tell you!" the giant computer bellowed. "You have to find it for yourself!

Remember, always, the saying: the pen is mightier than the sword!"

Then a swiping, swishing, cutting sound was heard coming towards them, they looked in the direction it was coming from, wide-eyed, expecting.

"Figure it out, you two!" the giant computer-screen bellowed. "Remember the pen, the mighty pen!" and the giant computer disappeared.

"The Pen! The Pen!" Sidney shouted. And they saw a giant pen coming towards them.

"The Pen can make us free. The Pen is going to make him free!"

The sky darkened. Thunder rumbled!

"Let`s fly!" Sidney put his arms around Reavis` shoulder and they flew away like birds.

Giant pens appeared writing words in the air, on leaves, on tree-trunks, words Sidney couldn`t understand nor decipher. He was using extrasensory power trying to penetrate the meanings.

"Our lives are mapped out in pages", Sidney said finally, coming out of a deep concentration. "All the pages are correctly numbered."

Reavis felt light like a feather.

"Keep the faith in the imagination of King and all will be right," Sidney called out.

"Dreams come true."

Reavis` eyes were tightly shut but his face was smiling.

Faraway they heard a great crash and an explosion as they rose higher and higher over the forest.

"Open your eyes now, Professor," Sidney said soothingly. "All is well. We are safe."

Reavis opened his eyes and said, "What was that great noise? Is it going to affect us?"

"No, professor. Remember your faith in King," replied Sidney as they sailed away across the brightest, bluest sky.

19

They landed on a farm in the English country-side. The farmer, a tall, red-faced man, and his wife, a plump woman with a round face and fading blonde hair, greeted them amongst some sheep.

"Oh, dear, look at what we got here!" the farmer said to his wife in a strange voice. And to Sidney and Reavis, "Where did you spring from?"

Reavis looked around at the farm and then at the farmer and his wife, and said sharply, "We fell from the sky and that`s the honest truth."

The farmer and his wife began to laugh. "You`re two of those comedian-chaps, aren`t you?" the farmer said. "Things like that only happen on television, in the movies or in fairy-tales."

"Yes, they are from fairy-tales," the farmer`s wife said and laughed uncontrollably. She stopped and blurted out, "Or, they must be flying around in one of those big balloon-things." As she laughed and spoke her whole body shook.

And you`re the weirdest farming couple I`ve ever encountered, Reavis thought.

"My name is Sidney Prince, and my companion`s name is professor Reavis," Sidney`s manner was gracious and relaxed. "Where are we? What is this place called?"

"A Prince and a Professor, my, my, we are honoured to make your acquaintances, sirs," the farmer stroked a lamb and bowed to Sidney and Reavis. His wife nodded, smiling. "You`re welcome to our humble abode."

Reavis was struck by the comical, unafraid behaviour of the farmer and his wife.

Sidney eyed them closely, "Thank you very much." he said, his eyes slanted. "We`ve come a very long way."

"Yes, your Highness," the farmer went on pleasantly, "I`m called Poeman. "And this is my wife, Tabita."

Tabita curtseyed and smiled.

Their names seemed familiar, Reavis thought. Sidney thought the same.

The sheep looked at Sidney and Reavis as if they too understood what was going on.

Reavis looked at the odd-looking animals suspiciously.

"We have pigs, chickens, ducks, horses, turkeys and a few cattle!" Poeman waved his hands in a wide sweep which took in a panoramic view of a nearby stream, hills, trees and an area of grazing cattle, chicken-runs, pig-pens and an area where the soil was recently tilled.

"We plant corn, wheat, barley, tomatoes, lettuce, cabbage, strawberries, apples and pears," Tabita put in joyfully.

Poeman led them to a large wooden table with wooden chairs near to some apple-trees, and said, "Would you like some cider? You must be thirsty after your long journey?"

"Yes, please, that would be nice," Sidney was charming.

But Reavis was doubtful and uneasy, and this was detected by Poeman and his wife.

"Is something wrong?" Poeman turned to Reavis as Tabita went off to get the cider.

Reavis didn`t know what to say, "Do you run this farm all by yourselves?" came out shakily.

"We have some men who help us," Poeman smiled, "they`re not here yet."

Reavis wasn`t satisfied, he sensed something else.

"We rarely get visitors in this part of the world. And certainly never as distinguished as yourselves."

Tabita returned with a wooden tray, a clay jug, two glasses and what looked like home-made biscuits. She placed the tray on the table and curtseyed again.

Reavis thought Tabita looked rather ridiculous, he sat at the table, looked at the tray, then at the couple again and at Sidney who sat beside him.

Poeman and Tabita stood watching them closely.

"Why don`t you two sit with us?" Reavis asked, almost snapping at them. "After all, it`s your place. And, by the way, my friend here, isn`t royalty. It`s just his family name. Like King isn`t a monarch, but the name of an outstanding writer."

"Thank you, sir," Poeman and Tabita said together and slowly sat down. "Last year there was a literature festival near here," Poeman went on, "book-writers from all over the world.

I remember now. They came and talked about how they invent their books."

"A lot of people came to see and hear them," Tabita put in, smiling. "We gave some of them lodgings. Otherwise, they put up tents and others camped in the open fields because it was a very hot summer for the whole week they were here."

"We were sad when it was finished, because we made many friends with some of them," Poeman said with sense of loss. "They were so kind and understanding. They never mocked us. Never laughed at us nor looked at us as odd folks." Reavis felt guilty, he poured a glass of cider and sipped, "Well, thank you for the cider. It`s delicious, tasty. I like it." He took a biscuit and munched, sipping and eating and forcing a smile, "Nice biscuits too. I appreciate your hospitality."

Sidney poured out a little cider, sipped and nodded, "Yes, very nice," he smilingly approving. But he didn`t partake of the biscuits. He was deep in thought.

Reavis began to feel strange, his head began to spin, in fact, everything began to spin as if he was drunk or caught in a whirlwind. He stood up, looked queerly at Sidney, swayed but maintained his balance.

Poeman and Tabita smiled at each other.

"Your friend has caught some kind of influence," Poeman said to Sidney.

Sidney put the glass down on the table, rose, held Reavis by the shoulder and calmed him and they both sat back down.

"You`re a powerful believer, Mr Prince, sir," Poeman said to Sidney. "You seem so sure of yourself."

"You and your wife seem to be under some kind of spell," Sidney stood again and addressed them. "I say again,

I`m looking for my favourite writer who is also my visionary companion. Some jealous force evil has been using a plot from one of his books to hold him captive. I can`t locate where he`s held. His signals to me are faint."

"Maybe the poor man is dead or dying," Tabita`s voice trembled. "We know about him."

"We heard about him," Poeman sighed greatly. As Poeman and Tabita spoke, the animals made sounds as if they were cheering them on.

Sidney sipped his cider, now took a biscuit and began to eat slowly. "Ah, yes, these biscuits are out of this world."

Reavis felt refreshed, relaxed and happy and began eating more biscuits and drinking cider, and giving the farmers a strange look, said, "The spell the two of you are under must have completely overwhelmed you!" then he smacked his lips.

"Well, we don`t have television and computers," Poeman`s voice was firm. "We read and tell stories our parents and grandparents told us. We remember childhood fairytales. I`m sure you know, Peter Pan, Hansel and Gretel, Jack and the Beanstalk and Cinderella." He stopped, took a deep breath, smiled, "Oh, we love listening to stories."

Tabita`s face lit up with the brightest glow, "You must be very careful in what you`re doing," her voice was suddenly frightened. "We read Stephen King too."

Sidney and Reavis looked at each other, puzzled.

"You see, Stephen King`s kidnapping is a warning to all writers about fame and celebrity and what it can cost the writer. Jealousy can breed evil." Poeman was deeply sad.

Reavis drained his glass, poured out more cider, sipped and studied the faces of Poeman and Tabita very carefully.

The animals cheered in animal noises!

"Well, what clues can you give us as to the whereabouts of King?" Reavis` eyes seemed to penetrate Poeman and his wife.

Then Poeman spoke in a voice which seemed not to be his own, "We don`t know, but Our clue to give is: never walk in the street, always keep on the kerb or side-walk. Whoever is holding him, is using a kind of radar and CCTV. And most important of all, keep a pen filled with ink in your pocket at all times."

Sidney was relieved and satisfied.

"Simply extraordinary!" Reavis winced.

Then Poeman and Tabita rose and moved away from the table, "Follow us to the barn!" Poeman commanded. "Come on, we trust you!"

Sidney and Reavis jumped up excitedly and followed the two farmers to a nearby barn: the doors of the barn flew open as Poeman approached and they went inside; there were no hay nor farming tools inside the barn, only a huge movie screen on one side. Tabita stood at the side of the giant movie screen as her husband pressed a light-switch and on the movie-screen was the figure of a person all bandaged from head to feet like an Egyptian mummy, limping and waving its arms.

Sidney was thinking hard.

Reavis` eyes popped and trembled, his heart raced, "Who the hell is that?" he spat out, his teeth knocking.

"We don`t know for sure," Poeman answered, his face in a troubled look.

"We suspect the person wrapped up like a mummy might be Stephen King," Tabita`s voice was tearful and afraid. "Whoever has him captive, wants him to give them his talents and success."

Reavis shook violently.

Poeman`s face was tragic. His wife was the same.

Sidney studied the mummy`s wrappings, his eyes seeming to xray the movie-screen, searching, searching.

Shivers went through their spines.

"King is trying to get through but his signals are so weak to us," Poeman was distressed.

"Tabita and I can`t make head nor tail of the signals. I mean, we feel we are his guardians, but we can`t do anything if his clues are so weak."

"I know," Sidney felt their sorrow and disappointment.

"He`s not held captive in England," Tabita was utterly distraught. "He`s underground somewhere, that`s for sure. You know, the novel, Misery was a warning to all successful authors."

"I know that," said Sidney thoughtfully. "It was my first thought. I`m going to find King if it means the end of my life."

They all stared at him.

Sidney was also very angry.

Reavis felt feverish but manage to hide his feelings.

"We were in America last year," Poeman said, his voice now losing all of its early happines and spark. "In his home-town, Bangor, Maine. But we didn`t pick up any clues from there."

"We didn`t either," said Sidney. "I`ll search the entire world to find King. He`s alive," Sidney`s voice wasn`t only confident but powerful and true.

Reavis brightened.

"Well, good luck to you both," Poeman and Tabita said together.

"My search may take me to heaven or hell and to regions undreamt of in any earthly Philosophy," said Sidney boldly. "But with the faith in King`s work and the emotions I find there in, I shall never falter nor be afraid."

The mummy-wrapped figure on the vast movie-screen, waved at the four of them, mumbled something, but Sidney couldn`t make it out: it sounded like a moan, a rhyme, a song, then the mummy-figure limped about in a kind of jigging dance, fell over and the vast movie-screen blurred and went out.

"What happened to it?" Reavis snapped, his eyes straining.

"That`s all we get," Poeman replied sadly. "And that`s our secret."

"It`s still something very important," Sidney was reassured. "You`re great guardians of the King."

It`s like a game of chess, Reavis thought.

"And we`re always very careful," Tabita said quickly. "We keep an eye on the movement of everyone coming near our farm. I`m sure there`re people like us in other parts of the world. And that makes us very satisfied."

"It makes me satisfied and happy as well," Sidney said triumphantly.

"We will always be here whenever you need our help," Poeman and Tabita were smiling again and this time their faces shone like the sun, lighting up the barn.

20

It was an evening in June; rain poured ceaselessly. Stephanie was in a large house somewhere in a country-side in a country she couldn`t make out. The house was like a castle, and she was in a bedroom standing by a window looking out at the rain, the colour of the surroundings, trees, and listening to the call of birds and other animals in the wet weather. The atmosphere was misty, but the mist seemed to move and had an intelligence as it moved from the fields of brown and green bushes and trees, wonderfully manicured lawn flowers of every colour and description, a fountain and a meadow; the mist moved around and over the entire great house, tapping at window-panes and huge doors. Birds now squawked; foxes, voles deer, squirrels, shrieked as the mist wrapped its arms around the entire country-side.

Inside the bedroom, it was warm, cosy and comfortable. Stephanie couldn`t make out what was going on with the vast mist. She felt a great pity for the animals outside caught in the rain and strange mist. She couldn`t understand how she got where she was, couldn`t identify the great castle or house. As the fingers of the mist tapped on the window, surprisingly, she wasn`t afraid but curious. The heavy rain stopped, and she heard a voice through the great mist which was more like a chant:

"In the Cave of mysterious shadows
Where it seems there are no tomorrows
If the winds bring news of creative writing
Here windows open to my handwriting!"

It had a sweet intoxicating melody. Stephanie heard it in her soul, her whole being swam in the delicious sea of honeyed tones. Its code, she thought, has to be deciphered. She tried to open the window, first it seemed jammed or stuck, then it gave way and opened with a rusty sound. She poked her head out, and the mist caressed her face, seeming to kiss her, she smiled then giggled uncontrollably, then she asked, "Who are you? What is all this? Why are you hiding in this mist?"

At first, the voice or the chant came from far away across the meadow, then from the fingers of the mist caressing Stephanie`s face:

"Search the forest of your mind
Leave the doubts and fears behind
In the centre of forgotten tombs
Therein the greatest treasure looms!"

"I`m sorry.......I.....I......I cannot understand it," Stephanie tried her sincerest best. "You`ll have to give me more time to decipher this clue. I`ll do my utmost best. Please, have patience with me." She felt helpless and that she was letting down Sidney and the others.

But the voice/chant from the mist soothed her with, "Don`t despair, Stephanie! You are unique and brave.

We are all over the world, reading stories of brave and bold!"

The building shook, swayed then steadied. Stephanie maintained her balance by clinging to the window-sill.

"What is this place? Where am I?" She managed. "How did I get here? I was with companions.!"

"One thing at a time!" the misty voice replied. "Your friend and companion are safe and well. You were brought here by the stretch of your imagination, fuelled by the King! This is a safe house. No one can penetrate its security net. And you are in Hereford, England. It`s beautiful, isn`t it!"

"Yes, yes, it`s beautiful countryside," Stephanie stuttered then relaxed.

The mist came through the window, then the window closed tight again, then it circled the room, seemingly searching, then it materialised into a limping, faceless man wearing a blue corduroy suit, black-and-white striped shirt and white sneakers.

"Time, that most valuable commodity in human life, is running out!" the faceless man said, turning to face Stephanie. "Time is running out for the KING! He is trapped! He cannot get organised thoughts through now! The jealous, evil one is punishing him!"

"We are searching everywhere," Stephanie didn`t mean to be angry. "My companions and I are putting everything into our search for King, but we so far we are coming up against barriers, invisible and otherwise!"

"Yes, I am aware of all that," the faceless man`s voice was tired and hoarse.

"Who are you?" Stephanie was impatient. "Don`t keep me in suspense any longer. Are you hiding?"

"I am from the imagination of a Stephen King story!" the faceless man waved his hands over his faceless front, and faces began to appear: red, black, purple, pink, yellow and multicoloured.

Stephanie`s eyes strained in amazement and wonder!

"Faces are masks of the true lives," the faceless man continued, conjuring the faces into every possible colour and also mixed colours. "It is what is in the brain that counts as the most important of all. The storyteller uncovers everything hiding behind the masks. The imagination fires the brain to create. Look, young lady, feast your eyes on the magic of the imagination!" And the faceless man began to change into different figures: animals, insects, clowns, naked men and women, babies, snarling dogs, six-gun-pistols with eyes, beings with several eyes and heads, beings from other planets, beings with no limbs only huge faces with huge eyes, beings with only hands and feet, and computers, type-writers and pens writing in many languages. "Faces! Take your pick of the masquerade!" the faceless man resumed his original shape and guise. "Search in this masquerade for your clues! I have already communicated with Prince and the others." Then the faceless man changed back into the mist again. "Some of the clues are to be found in some of King`s stories. Search carefully! Every life in the world can be a story of mystery and wonder! In a way, life is a giant movie!"

The room began to spin again with the mist circling Stephanie; a wind ruffled her hair and was strong enough to rip off all her clothes, she stood there naked and startled with her hands covering her private parts.

"You`re not cold?" the voice from the mist asked. "Prepare yourself for the ultimate journey of your life! Into infinite possibilities with King at the helm!" And the mist swirled around, faster and faster. The window snapped open and the mist went out, chanting, "Remember me! Remember me! You came into this world naked and so you shall leave it! I have already told the others to beware of false faces. Look beyond the masks! Get into the soul. Good luck! Have faith!" And the mist vanished. The rain ceased, the sky brightened and birds chirped merrily in green trees.

The room disappeared, the castle disappeared and Stephanie was left standing in the bright, fresh June evening in a meadow in an English country-side. She was fully-dressed. She heard voices coming towards her, she looked in their direction, straining, feeling a little afraid, but the voices sounded familiar, friendly, happy. She hurried in their direction, starlight sparkling on her face; as she drew near, the voices, excitedly, she recognised Sidney`s, William`s and Reavis` as they ran and embraced and kissed her passionately, their faces dazzling with smiles.

"Read every page of life around you very carefully!" Sidney exclaimed.

"Here! Here! Reavis beamed.

Stephanie felt an awakening deep in her soul.

William`s heart leapt almost out of his chest.

Sidney`s face radiated strange lights, "We have forged ourselves into a new family, an unbreakable bond in our services for the King. It`s a very great sacrifice. I must also tell you this, we don`t have to take in food through our mouths. All we have to do is think hard about delicious food and drink and we`ll be filled and satisfied. All this is through the imagination of King!"

Already they felt filled and contented. Sunshine danced on their faces and the sky was smilingly blue.

"Let`s get going!" Sidney said confidently.

Once again they hugged and kissed each other.

"Do you know that King`s accident changed the way he walked?" Sidney said suddenly.

They nodded.

"That`s one of the most important clues or signposts," Sidney went on, "keep that in mind always."

"The limping figure wrapped up like a mummy on the giant movie-screen in the barn on that farm," they all said together and looked searchingly at each other.

"Keep alert at all times!" Sidney breathed deeply as he spoke. "It`s becoming very dangerous! Expect the unexpected!"

"Your mind is certainly on fire," Reavis patted Sidney`s shoulder. "You are in full consciousness."

Their faces reflected the smiling sun.

"In and out of stories we go!" Sidney shouted, raising his hands in the air.

"Here we go! Here we go again!" the others answered.

And they all disappeared, and reappeared in a small town east of the place called Cumberland, twenty miles north of a place called Portland. They all shivered a little except Sidney who seemed to know exactly where he was going. They walked along a deserted street, stopped in front of a large what looked like an empty mansion. Sidney pointed at the building. The others stared wide-eyed and expectant.

"It looks like a haunted house from one of King`s stories!" William bit his lip.

"Let`s start here in our search!" Sidney said, leading them to the mansion.

It was an ominous evening, cold, the sky was dark.

"We`re certainly sticking to details," Reavis commented, looking at and around the mansion.

They all kept their nerves.

"We cannot give away any hint as to what we are about as there might be spies in all kinds of disguises," Sidney warned, first knocking, then after thirty minutes, pushing the great door which yielded to his force.

The door opened with a great painful creak.

"We`re in vampire territory," Reavis said, his voice seemed to echo. "Salem`s Lot, I imagine.

How long do we have to be here?" as they followed Sidney; Reavis` legs felt lifeless.

"This house hasn`t been lived in for centuries," Stephanie muttered, following, with William bringing up the rear.

A shadow passed over their faces.

"The length of time we stay here will depend on what we find to help us in our quest,"

Sidney answered as he made his way into a huge dusty, hallway with rooms leading off.

"I wonder how many floors are there," Stephanie speculated, grimacing.

"Could be at least seven floors," Reavis said thoughtfully. "This building has been here since feudal and colonial times. It has all kinds of entrances, exits, rooms leading everywhere, secret and otherwise."

I believe there are more than enough rooms to accommodate us down here."

"We`re going to occupy the ground floor," Sidney announced. "Each of us can take a room.

There was a great fire-place where a fire blazed.

They began searching around for a room to please each one of them. They found five rooms, large, spacious and dusty. There were a dilapidated bathroom with a fire-place and eighteen-century style furnishings in all the rooms, the walls and the rugs on the floors.

"It`s most likely haunted," William whispered to himself. But the others picked it up.

They met again in the kitchen-area, and Sidney said, "The beds in the rooms haven`t been slept in for a long time."

"We noticed that," the others said together.

"I doubt I`ll be doing much sleeping," Reavis said, looking around the ancient kitchen.

"Well, in case any of us feel incline," Sidney looked at William and Stephanie and smiled.

"It`s a very strange place," William said, also looking around the kitchen. "It`s as if it was prepared for us," his voice trailing off.

Then there was a shriek, they turned and Stephanie was staring at a poster in a corner: They came and investigated the poster which advertised: "The New York Review of Books in conjunction with the Times Literary Supplement, a lecture on the Creative Imagination of Lovecraft."

"I don`t understand......could this be the same Lovecraft?" Stephanie asked, looking intently at Sidney.

"I`m not so sure about that," Sidney answered, examining the poster carefully.

"Maybe a distant relative, perhaps," William ventured.

"I don`t think so," Reavis put in, shaking his head. "Remember everything is possible in our present situation."

"Let`s check the cellar or basement!" Sidney called. "I`m sure there are several."

The floors and rooms and the hallways were covered with worn-out Persian carpets and rugs.

"Yes! let`s!" Reavis said contemplating the floor.

They searched all over the ground floor, some floorboards were wood-wormed, others creaky and rotted.

The sky darkened, ominous clouds blotted out a moon trying to peep through.

Cries and howls of wolves and people were heard outside the mansion. The four looked at each other quizzically but weren`t afraid. Then Sidney`s fingers found hinges in the creaky floor in a corner of one of the rooms, he tapped, ripped away the worn rotting carpet and saw a door which he thought must lead underground to a cellar or basement, he lifted the door and it almost came apart in his hands with a groaning tear.

Looking down, they saw steps leading down into darkness, deep and foreboding.

"I`ll go down first and check," Sidney said and began to descend the steps carefully.

The others waited in wonder.

"We`ll await your call," Reavis spoke and the others nodded.

Outside the moon finally peeped through the dark clouds, and the wolves howled louder!

"Professor, you will come down when I call!" Sidney said. "Stephanie and William can remain up there and keep watch!"

The howling of the wolves seemed now to come from inside the mansion.

"Listen to them," William remembered Bram stoker`s Dracula: "the children of the night", he quoted.

"We`re not going to let that put us off our watch," Stephanie said bravely.

Sidney descended deep into the underground, then called Reavis who came down very carefully. The atmosphere was cold, chilling and mouldy with rotten corpses.

Sidney`s flashlight surveyed the scene.

"This is a real hell-hole," Reavis` voice was full of darkness.

The floor of the basement or cellar was black earth mixed with seashells and pebbles. Sidney shone the light in corners which were large, and in one of the corners, his eyes managed to make out just what he suspected, a coffin. They moved about carefully, trying not to trip over corpses.

Reavis gasped, "But! How did you? I can`t understand!" Could this be the same Vampire`s house from the novel, "Salem`s Lot?""

"The Marsten`s house," Sidney answered, "I`m not sure, it might be a diversion," and he walked briskly and skilfully to the ancient-looking coffin, the flashlight bright as a full moon.

Reavis followed cautiously. Sidney handed the flashlight to him and said, "I`m going to open it and check. Please keep the light steady and focussed."

Reavis` fingers were sweaty as he took the flashlight and kept it steadily shining on the coffin.

Sidney, with all his might, lifted the lid which opened with a growling creak, inside was a man, but not an ageing man but a young man in his late teens.

"But, but.....in ...the book...the master vampire was a decaying old monster."

Reavis said roughly, "This is a youth with a face like angel. I don`t understand it."

"Be patient, Professor, all will be revealed in time," Sidney assured him. "Youth can be deceptive as you know."

The two men stared at the youth lying in the coffin. Reavis` heart raced, then he relaxed.

Sidney had a cunning mischievous look.

"You`ll remember in the novel, some of the youngsters were vampires or had become so," Sidney took the deepest of breaths, leaning over the coffin which was new, his face near the white youthful face of the figure. "Youth is another signpost we have to look out for, Professor.Now we have first, the limping man, and then this youth about nineteen lying in a vampire lair. And also, you will remember King writing somewhere that nineteen is the best or the most interesting age, at that age, the world is seen as the person`s oyster. The teenage-mantle is thrown off. At nineteen, one is about to embark on all the promises and ambitions of childhood."

"You speak like a very wise old person."

The winds howled and the wolves growled louder and louder!

"Let`s go back upstairs," Sidney said, replacing the lid of the coffin.

The entire building shook. Reavis almost fell over.

"The vampires are very angry tonight," Sidney`s voice was steady as it echoed throughout the scene. "This building is just a smoke-screen, a kind of disguise."

The building began to spin, slowly, then fast, faster, faster, but none of the four lost their balance, they stood erect and solid as the insides of the building whirled around like a tornado. Sidney began smilingly to hum a rock-and –roll tune, then shouted, "We cannot be touched in this quest!"

The building suddenly stopped spinning. Reavis and Sidney looked at each other. Stephanie and William did the same. Sidney`s face was glowing like a full moon.

"Let`s go to our rooms, but don`t take them as real," Sidney instructed his companions as he and Reavis came up from the mysterious underground cellar. "Let's go and have a rest for all its worth. Everything is going as I expected. We'll find the rooms lit, warm and comfortable."

They stared at him, believing and fascinated.

They found their rooms just as Sidney described: the beds were made, candles burned in chandeliers, each room was warm and comfortable. Before they fell asleep, they heard screams of children, adults, accompanied by the howling wolves and the fluttering of great wings. But they were contented and soothed by the fact that no harm could come to them.

Their sleep was dream-less.

Sidney awoke, he was lying on his back looking up at the ornate ceiling, thinking, then he muttered, "Oh, blasted spite, that I was born to put it right."

The building began to take off like a helicopter, up, up in the air, sprouting wings; a rock-and-roll band was heard playing loudly all over the flying building. The building hovered over and around the scene, then exploded, and voices of the rock-and-roll band sang: "Salem's Lot!

Salem's Lot! That's all we got! That's all we got!" And a guitar whined!

Now the sun was shining dazzlingly bright. Sidney and his companions weren't hurt nor injured. Their faces always shone in darkness. They were on the roof of the University of Maine. A feather-pen, a typewriter, a computer-word-processor, appeared in front of them, hovering like a humming-bird; they stared at the computer-screen, and the face of Shakepeare appeared on the screen, speaking loud and clear: "We meet again! You are on the right track! I am coming through to you courtesy of Poeman`s and Tabita`s machine! And, yes, young Prince, you were born to set things right! These machines in your world keep on amazing me! I call them toys of the imagination. The real inventions are yet to come. I think they are somewhere in the seeds of Stephen King`s fiction. Farewell! Parting is such sweet sorrow! But who knows, we might meet tomorrow! Good luck!"

There were sunshine smiles on Sidney`s and his companions` faces.

"I knew the Bard was with us all along," said Reavis excitedly. "We`re firmly on the right path, yes, Mr. Prince, you`re a genius. The world must open the pages of every Stephen King story."

As the face of Shakespeare disappeared from the computer-screen, a limping figure, bandaged like a mummy took its place, wailing, "Tread carefully! Save me ! I`m real! This isn`t a disguise! Remember me!"

"Where are you speaking from?" Reavis asked. "Give us some kind of clue?"

"I don`t know!" came the reply from the bandaged mummy figure. "This is all I can say at the present time! I`m in the dark, struggling to get through this maze. Remember me, until we meet again!"

"Of course, I`ll remember you!" Sidney shouted "Alas, poor captive."

The sky darkened, thunder roared, winds began to howl, and red rain began to fall, pouring down; it was raining blood; a flood of blood surrounded them, spreading all over the area, coming up towards the roof.

"This is the blood of the Vampires!" Sidney shouted above the din, his face shining as usual. "Also this is the blood of Carrie. Remember the novel."

His companions nodded.

"We`re safe in the imagination of King," Sidney was standing erect as he spoke, smiling as the flood of blood rose; he waved a hand and the computer-screen disappeared. "Hold on to each other`s hand tightly!" he commanded.

Stephanie, Reavis and William held on to each other`s hands, Sidney joined and they made a circle. "This is a beautiful place," Sidney said, his voice sweet and melodic. "The strength of youth and the wisdom of the old are in the book. Together they are the most powerful force. Our quartet must never be broken. We must go now, move on." And Sidney and his companions disappeared from the roof of the University of Maine.

21

Sidney and his companions were hovering above a small town in America.

"Do you think he`s somewhere here?" Reavis asked, surveying the small mid-western town"Remember never to speak out loud where we are," Sidney again warned. "King`s captors aren`t careless."

William shrugged.

Sidney was in the deepest thoughts.

"What are we looking for here? Stephanie seemed impatient.

Early morning sunshine spotlighted their eager shining faces as they floated around. primroses, daisies, tulips, apple and pear trees geranium, chickadee, blueberry, larks and eagles, swayed in breezes on hedgerows, fences; sang as they flew: the scenes were sensual and breath-taking.

"My dear, friends, there clues within clues, and the clues, I suspect, will be few." Sidney said, his eyes penetrating the surroundings. "It is not only in the books we are going to find clues. And it`s not going to be easy. We have to keep vigil."

"We realise that," the three said together.

"Great," Sidney was smiling and shining.

"This whole business is like a puzzle," Stephanie said thoughtfully.

"In a way, we are in a kind of an epic novel," Sidney mused.

"Captured, you mean by an invisible author?" Reavis suggested.

"Not one of King`s stories?" said William, looking around wildly.

"No, no, we could be in a story of our own making," Sidney said, looking at them penetratingly. "We are not captured by anybody, no. "

The sun filled their faces with hope.

"The price of fame can be dangerous," Sidney said solemnly.

"J.K. Rowling better watch out," Stephanie gasped. "The Green-eyed monsters are everywhere."

Reavis nodded and turned away.

"We need a key to open the door of discover the secret of our quest," Sidney announced brightly. "There are many roads. We have to choose the right ones or we`ll lose King."

His companions nodded.

"King`s novel, Carrie, was set here," Sidney went on. "For me, it represents youth and blood, life-blood, if you like."

"Yes, I see it," Reavis confirmed.

The others smiled, "Yes."

The sun now blazed brighter than ever.

The scene shifted to another place and another time.

Sidney couldn`t make out the place, the seasons changed rapidly.

"Are we lost?" William inquired, his voice seemed to echo.

Stephanie and Reavis stared at each other.

Sidney`s eyes were radiating their strange beams. "I`m sure you`ll remember the character, John Smith in the novel, Dead Zone. He had an accident and was able to see the evil in people."

"Is that the clue or key?" asked Reavis strongly.

"King can see deep into the evil of people in his stories," Sidney continued. "Before his accident, and more so, after the accident, he saw deepest."

"I see it!" Stephanie exclaimed.

"Me too," William joined her.

Robins, finches and gaily-coloured butterflies rode the air-waves.

They were certainly outside linear time and were now in a higher state of consciousness.

"The jealous evil thing that kidnapped King," Sidney began with a cunning smile, "cannot kill him, because it knows that King can see beyond everyday life of this world, and they` re holding him captive in this world, in this dimension. He can see through masks and disguises."

"Yes! Yes!" Reavis was excited. "I fully understand."

"We are all clear," Sidney surveyed them closely.

"King isn`t going to be killed!" they were overjoyed.

Sidney`s face was over-flowing with wonder.

"Why do you think we are her?" Reavis asked Sidney, his voice morose.

"All that will be made clear soon," Sidney replied with very strong, confident tone. "We have to investigate the tiniest clues. Whether they are in the novels, Carrie, Salem`s Lot or The Dead Zone. We must seek beyond the meanings in these stories."

Suddenly there was a sound like that from a mobile-phone. They looked at each other.

"Whose mobile is that?" Sidney asked, his face registering a worry. "Please, no mobiles on our journey. I thought I made that abundantly clear. Things like that can be traced."

His companions shook their heads violently.

Then a voice from above them like an over-voice on television or movie-screen, said, "I`m Lovecraft! I`m sorry if I startled you! Sometimes look for similarities in some of the stories! For example, there`s a writer called Ben in Salem`s Lot, and of course, the kidnapped writer in Misery, and the writer who was killed in Lisey`s Story. Then the importance of a quest which is the basis of The Dark Tower books. But don`t only depend on these, follow your instincts!"

"We understand!" Sidney and his companions answered together, looking up at what was sky and now ceiling and then sky again.

"The pen is indeed mightier than any weapon!" the voice of Lovecraft cried out. "The pen answers all riddles. Jealousy and evil can never hide!"

There was a crash! Like that of an accident involving vehicles, screeching of tyres, a bang! a wail!

"Oh, what a terrible time that was when he thought he had died!" the voice from above swooned. " Accidents can extinguish life, can open up areas of being, areas of creative energy beyond belief!"

Above them stars shone in a golden sky and there were new constellations. They felt new strengths pulsing through their bodies.

"You are ready for anything and everything!" the voice of Lovecraft boomed. "I`m pleased or indeed, we`re pleased! The characters in every King`s stories are keeping a watchful eye on the four of you! Be careful how you read!"

Reavis thought about asking a question but decided against it. William felt light-headed but contented. Stephanie was enchanted.

"What about the test?" Sidney asked, his voice full of purpose.

"Yes, Prince. I haven`t forgotten that!" said the voice from what was now an ornate ceiling high above. "You are going to enter areas of unimaginable evil! If you become weak, afraid or lose faith, you will be swept away! If you are not strong in soul, mind and body, you will touched by the jealous evil hand and crushed. My voice has the greatest buzz of human life!"

"We are always ready. We heed all these warnings," Sidney said strongly.

His companions chanted, "Yes!"

"I`m many voices in many roles!" the voice went on. "Off you go, then!" Then the voice silent.

"Let it be," they whispered together.

The changing surroundings disappeared and Sidney and his friends were in a desert, the sun was beating down, unbearably hot. Their throats were parched and tight.

"Save me! Save me!" they heard a voice from behind them wailing. "The four of you must save me!"

They turned around and saw a woman, middle-aged, coming towards them, "I`m Atibat!" she sobbed, wringing her hands, her body twisting like a snake. "They`ve taken my man! They are going to kill him! Oh, God, I think they want to eat him! They want to get his strength!

What has happened to the literary world! Help me! Please, save him! Save us!" The woman was near to them now,her face seemed familiar but they couldn`t remember where they had seen her.

"Who has taken your man?" Sidney asked surveying the woman.

The others also surveyed her.

"I can`t remember," answered the woman. "Because they have turned me inside out. You have to unravel this mystery."

"We have heard your name before, but your face has changed," Reavis said, looking intently at Sidney.

"Yes, the name," Stephanie and William uttered together

"Changed inside out, yes, I see," said Sidney thoughtfully. "Where have you come from?"

"Solve me, help me, young Prince," the woman shrieked. "This is a supreme test. If you don't solve it, you're doomed!"

The sun was punishingly hot blazing their faces but not Atibat's.

"Quick, Prince! Otherwise you aren't going anywhere and you'll die of thirst and hunger which you'll soon begin to feel!" As Atibat spoke her body shook.

And indeed, Sidney and his friends began to experience thirst, their throats were raw and burning.

"Doomed! We can't be doomed!" Reavis bawled.

"Hurry and solve this riddle, Prince!" Atibat commanded.

Stephanie and William held their throats. Reavis rubbed his chest violently.

Sidney stood erect but trembled, "Of course, Atibat, you have been turned inside out!" he said bravely, "Yes, I have it. Your name spelt backwards is, TABITA, King's wife. It is spelt Tabitha, but we have as, Tabita. That is it. I've solved it." he felt fine, not thirsty nor hungry.

His friends were relieved, satisfied and smiling.

"And this desert we've crossed, is the same desert in the novel, The Dark Tower," Sidney was very happy. "I've solved it. Yes, my friends, we did it!"

Atibat or Tabitha had disappeared; the desert also disappeared.

"Keep on with the strong faith, hold on to your beings tightly," Sidney lovingly said to his companions.

The scorching sun became cool and was now smiling on them. They heard a faraway voice soothingly saying,

"You have passed the test! Go on our quest! Remember, King has empowered even his weakest characters with extraordinary talents!"

"We`re always ready!" Sidney sang out bravely.

They all felt rejuvenated with a new sense of purpose, a new sense of time and place.

"We`ve done very well so far," Sidney smiled radiantly at his friends, his eyes emitting a rainbow.

Reavis felt like a completed new man; Stephanie felt like she wanted to go to a toilet and William felt he could do anything.

"Check your body-parts to see if they are all there in the right places," Sidney said, checking his own being. "We must still use telepathy."

"I am satisfied," Reavis remarked smilingly.

They closed their eyes for some minutes in deep meditation.

"Yes, everything is all right," William and Stephanie said together.

"We aren`t a hundred per cent there yet," said Sidney, "but our minds are opened for an objective sense of knowing, not a subjective sense. This is objective consciousness." He waved his hands in the air, and suddenly they were in a 1950`s chevolet-car driven by Sidney. Stephanie was beside and Reavis and William were in the back.

"Where are we going?" Reavis asked, rocking from side to side.

"I`m not completely sure but we`re on the right track," as he spoke Sidney`s eyes were on a very busy street in a city in the United States. His eyes were piercing the surroundings down to the smallest detail.

The car was speeding but Sidney was in total control, contentment shone on his face.

Reavis and the others were also surveying the scene.

"We`re in very good hands, Professor!" Stephanie said gaily.

The car zoomed through the traffic. Horns blew! Engines roared! There were shouts from motorists. Then suddenly, it all went dark and vehicles crashed into Sidney`s 1950`s car.

"Accident! Accident!" a voice rang out from the wreckage. "It`s my accident, not yours! On your way! You aren`t hurt!"

The 1950`s chevolet disappeared from the scene, and Sidney and his companions found themselves walking down Times Square.

"By George, that was close," Reavis said, looking around.

"That accident wasn`t for us, only a warning," Sidney remarked, taking a deep breath and straightening himself.

Passers-by eyed them suspiciously.

"Whose voice was that?" William asked, his hair fallen over his face.

"Can`t you guess," said Stephanie who was unruffled.

22

A hurricane wind came and swept them up and away in blue sky. They went up and up into the blue beyond. They weren`t afraid nor surprised.

"Aha, the Quest quartet!" A voice called to them. "Get ready for wonders of the creative genius of the King. Good luck!"

A cloud floated by, and Sidney sat on it and invited the others to do the same. They obeyed.

"It`s safe and solid as a rock or an armchair," Sidney smiled. They agreed.

"You know," William began, staring down at the now tiny American scenery. "I somehow feel the safest I`ve ever felt."

"Some of the excellent writers living today haven`t received the Nobel Prize, Reavis mused.

"That`s true, I wonder why, maybe it`s connections " said William thoughtfully.

"King is his own man," said Stephanie firmly, "he writes what he likes and feels."

Sidney stretched his arms wide, his face was bright with conviction. The cloud sailed away smoothly. Sidney`s eyes were like flaming torches.

"You`re on fire, my lad," Reavis rose, looking into his eyes while he spoke; Sidney`s eyes seemed to be flowing out of their sockets like sunrays.

William and Stephanie stared at Sidney.

"I know, I know, come to me!" Sidney said to them, the eyes with sunrays streaming out.

They came to him and he embraced them tightly and each felt a warm current emanating from Sidney into their bodies, it was the sweetest, the most satisfying sensation they had ever experienced. They wanted to melt away in the wonderful fire.

The cloud disappeared from under and around them, and they entered a region of darkness. Everyone except Sidney stumbled about; Sidney seemed to know his way about the darkness.

"Follow my voice!" he called to them. "All will be well!"

They groped around but soon found their way in the direction of Sidney`s voice.

"Don`t be afraid, remember we are one always!" Sidney stressed, his eyes like a flashlight guiding them on.

The darkness cleared, and now they were hovering over Colorado in the United States.

A voice came into Stephanie`s head, saying, "Steph, girlie, where are you going? To find a lover or have a shit?"

The others pick it up and kept their eyes penetratingly on Stephanie who held head high and proud.

"What does it mean?" she said, looking at Sidney.

"Smile and take it easy, my dear," Sidney said charmingly. "Don`t let it put you off.

You`re doing fine."

Then it was William`s turn to hear a voice in his head, it said, "What do you want with all this searching, Billy boy? You have found your sweetness already. Give it up!" William rubbed his head vigorously and spat out, "The voice is speaking to me now! It`s chanting all over my brain!"

"You can take it. You are capable enough," Sidney said to him and he massaged William`s head gently. "You are all right.

They were now walking along an almost deserted street. William, staggered, blinked and said, "It...it...has left me."

Reavis suddenly shook, fell over on a nearby grassy pathway, his clothes began to be ripped from his body by invisible hands. He laid on his back, staring up at his companions who were gathered around him. "I felt fingers taking my clothes off," he stuttered. "Then the fingers rubbed my body. What`s it all about."

"Remain calm, you have the strength," Sidney said to him, rubbing his head while the retrieved his clothes which were in the street. "Think of your favourite Stephen King`s novel and all will be well."

"Yes, yes, yes, that`s it," Reavis relaxed, sat up, stood and put his clothes back on.

"You know, it the fingers felt like those of a woman, sexually massaging me.,making love to me."

And indeed, a woman`s voice whispered in Reavis` ear, "I`m Professor Prufuck. You remember we use to fuck in your study at Cambridge after discussing T.S.Eliot. We made love all through Ash Wednesday. You were a good Prufuck then."

"We heard it, Professor," the others said.

"I never had such an experience at my university," Reavis said, he was now sweating. "It`s the jealous evil force which is holding King playing with our heads."

That`s right. We must be stronger than ever," Sidney said, "It can play with our senses, use disguises and tricks but it cannot stop our quest."

"Mate me, Professor, please, mate me," the mysterious woman`s voice whispered again in Reavis` ear, then the voice materialised into an old woman with grey hair, dull blue eyes, buxom and completely naked.

"What!" Stephanie, William and Reavis said together, but Sidney calmly helped Reavis regained his feet.

The woman confronted them angrily, "Why are you meddling in things which do not concern you!"

Sidney and his friends looked at each other and thought deeply.

Reavis was relaxed.

"I am always watching over great writing and lovers of great storytelling!" the strong firm voice of the Bard, materialising into Shakespeare standing erect and proud before them, and the Bard was dressed in 20th century clothes, jeans, white long sleeved shirt and sneakers.

The old woman turned to Shakespeare and snarled, "Maybe if you knew how to fuck Anne Hattaway sweetly, you would`ve been the world`s greatest fucker instead of the world`s greatest dramatist and poet!"

"I did my best, Madam," Shakespeare responded calmly, and turning to Sidney, said, "Sweet Prince, this one is worse than Lady Macbeth. Handle her with the utmost care. She is pure evil."

"She`s like the monster which took possession of a side of Susannah in the Dark Tower book!" Sidney thought he had discovered another clue.

"You created some scoundrels in your time, Bard, bad!" the old woman, now sweating profusely, spat at Shakespeare. "You shouldn`t pass judgment on me!"

Reavis was the picture of bewilderment, his showed red anger.

"Yes, Bard boy, this is a dagger you see before you!" the old woman cried out, spitting blood. "And all the mother-fucking world is a bloody stage! And no quality of mercy is going is going to strained! This academic prick is going to Dante`s Hell!"

"How are you?" Sidney asked Reavis, stroking his shoulder gently.

"I`m all right, Prince," Reavis replied softly.

"That`s going to be difficult for the four of you seekers, wise-arse Prince!" the old woman snapped at Sidney. "This Professor is your weak link, he`ll break soon. He`s going to betray you!" And to Shakespeare, she snarled, "Now, you go to blazes!"

Reavis kept a sweating, tired brave face. Stephanie and William held him strongly in their thoughts.

"I am sure the Professor is going to be all right," Shakespeare was smiling at Reavis

"Your beloved King will never win the Nobel Prize!" the old woman crackled. "Professor, you tell them! You were the distinguished academic, tell them!" she spat at Reavis.

Reavis looked at her steadily and unflinching.

Darkness hovered above and around them, but the light from Sidney`s eyes guided them to see through the darkness.

"Leave us alone! Get thee hence!" William shouted at the old woman, his face flaming with anger.

The old woman cast a wicked look at him and raged, "What do you think, boy! Because you have same name as the Bard, you`re word-perfect with your threats! You force-ripe ponce!" her eyes were fiery.

William felt a shiver moving up and down his spine, but he kept his composure.

The darkness was trying to wrap them, but Shakespeare announced, clapping his hands, "Now, for a change of act and scene!" And Sidney and his companions were now looking at a scene on a stage of a play showing the old woman, still naked, beating a man with a whip; the man had a pen in his hand staggering around the stage; the old woman shouted, "Write what we want! Change it! Scene melt into scene! Let your pen give us life! The mighty pen started it all!"

Shakespeare disappeared.

Sidney and his friends stared at the display, and recognised the man with the pen being beaten, was none other than Stephen King or an apparition of King.

"We've found him!" Reavis exclaimed triumphantly.

"Yes! Yes!" Stephanie and William merrily said together.

"I'm afraid not," Sidney warned. " Let's have a good look at this scene and act. I might get more clues. Please, look for clues."

"I understand, yes," Reavis said slowly.

"Let's join hands in a chain and chant King's name!" Sidney commanded.

The four joined hands tightly in a circle and chanted loudly: "Stephen King! Stephen King!

Where are you? Stephen King! Stephen King! Let us sing!" Reavis was smiling widely.

"Oh, King, if we're in your imagination!" Sidney called out, "Write a clue for us! We're going to find you!"

The old woman, crazed, upright with hands akimbo, the whip on her shoulder, shouted, "I'll decide what he writes! Fuck art for art's sake! He'll write for my sake! We'll get you all!"

"We can't just watch and do nothing," William was impatient, turning to Sidney, he said, "King is suffering. There're going to change him."

"I can assure you, my friend," Sidney put an arm lovingly around William's shoulder and said, "That's not Stephen King there. It's one of the clever tricks of the kidnappers. Watch and try to get a clue from all this scene and act."

"Yes, I....I...I see it now, it's an act," William understood. The others concurred.

"Find the key! Find the clue to free me!" A voice echoed around them.

The old woman started beating the Stephen King character again, Fuck that! Fuck him!

Fuck that voice!"

"They`ll take on many disguises!" the voice echoed around them again. "You four can free me! You`re strong!"

Sidney and his companions now heard the voice speaking in the centre of their beings.

"Re-write the stories!" the old woman raged on the stage in make-believe scene and act, her hair wild and flying, her eyes blood-red, her face contorted mad wild beast, and then, her hair began to cover her entire body, now she was growling and snarling.

The Stephen King character on the stage began to limp around and the scene was changing into an underground cave with him sitting at a table with a computer, his head in his hands.

"Don`t whimper!" the old woman bawled at him. "The world isn`t going to end in any whimper!"

"This jealous evil force is extremely powerful," Stephen King spoke to Sidney and his friends inside their deepest selves. "They want me to give them my talent and popularity. Call out the names of some of my books loudly!"

Sidney and the others began to call out the names of some of King`s novels:

"CARRIE!" Reavis shouted at the top of his voice.

"IT!" shouted Stephanie.

"BAG OF BONES!" William called out.

Sidney was smiling all over.

"THE DEAD ZONE!" Reavis said strongly.

"SALEM`S LOT!" Sidney`s voice filled the scene.

"THE SHINING!" Stephanie shouted.

"THE STAND!" Reavis was enthusiastic. "And we`re making a mighty stand!"

"DREAMCATCHER!" Stephanie said with a thrill.

"That`s enough," King`s voice from inside them said with a strangeness.

Reavis sighed, deeply contented.

"And out of this darkness, where does it lead?" Sidney asked the voice inside him.

"Where does it lead?" his companions asked together.

Suddenly, Sidney had the answer forming in his mind as he said, "To the Dark Tower, yes, I get it now, yes. "All roads in the stories and novels lead to the Dark Tower," all this was told to his companions telepathically. They understood.

"I wonder what shit the four of you are thinking about!" the old woman raged, "You miserable creatures! I want all his glory! Where are the four of you going?"Then she whipped the make-believe character of King again and again, "Give me the glory! I`ll give you more than the Nobel Prize if your give me your genius!" A great black shroud covered her.

"That`s another aspect of the man in black," Sidney communicated to his companions.

"We realised that," they replied together.

The old woman dropped her whip and cuffed the make-believe Stephen King character behind his head. The computer-screen blinked," Write me! Write me!" the old woman howled and changed into a giant beetle, snorting fire.

The make-believe Stephen King character began working his fingers over the now blank computer-screen but nothing appeared.

"You mother-fucking dumb-head!" the old woman screamed. "What! Don`t tell me your imagination has gone! Don`t let those shits outside of our scene stop you!"

Suddenly, on the computer-screen, the words: "But they can learn" came on. The old woman quickly turned off the computer and placed a small typewriter in front of the make-believe King character and commanded, "Try this for size with no interference!" She slipped a blank sheet of typewriting paper in the machine and from her beetle-mouth, spat out, "When that is finished, I`ll get more paper!"

"In all the books we`ve named," Sidney communicated telepathically to his friends, "all the Evil was conquered.

They swam in the glow of this truth.

The make-believe Stephen King character began to type frantically, his eyes closed, sentences and paragraphs came on the sheet of paper that read: "There was an old woman who changed into a monster. She had a lot of nasty disguises, no one would believe her! She talked like a woman but thought as the monster inside her. Oh, dear me, she said, I`d rather be finished and dead!"

"What crap is that!" the old woman boomed, looking at what was typed out. Thunder struck the surroundings. "You think you can fool me! I want your glory! Or you`ll never write again! Write me into fame and glory! I want that dazzling imagination of yours!"

Reavis, Stephanie and William came together and held each other tightly so that their bodies fused into one as the thunder struck and bounced off them. Sidney understood. The three friends came apart again to their individual selves,enchanted.

The thunder ceased.

"I`m all those jealous frustrated critics rolled into one big green-eyed monster!" the old Woman screamed. "I WANT IT! I WANT IT! THE FIERY FAME!"

Sidney smiled glowingly and lit up the faces of his companions, brighter and clearer.

"You think I don`t know that you`re Richard Bachman!" the old woman laughed, turning back to her human form.

"Some writers take on different persona!" Sidney called out. "King has opened up regions of the imagination even monsters like you can`t imagine. BACHMAN is extension of himself. He wasn`t trying to hide. You must surrender to the powerful mind of King!"

"Never! Never!" the old woman raged and snorted red flames. "Not until he has given me fame!"

"Understand and appreciate, not understand and dominate!"Sidney shouted. "Creativity must never be forced nor bullied, it flows naturally!"

"Don`t interfere, you four, keep out of it!" she boomed. "Fuck off from the scene! But.... but....but....why.....do....I...I.. feel so funny. I`m changing....without me doing it. What`s happening......to me!........Oh, vanity....all is our vanity!"

The make-believe Stephen King character smiled and waved at Sidney and his companions, and then wrote on the computer-screen: "You are on the right track" which only they could see.

"He`s getting through," Sidney and his friends communicated to each other.

The old woman staggered about the stage-scene, fell over, trembling, bawling, "All right! All right, but it`s not over yet, it`s not so easy. You`re not getting away so easy!"

"Let`s go from this hellish sight," Sidney said to his companions, his voice was cheerful.

The old woman disappeared in a puff of black smoke,and the image of the make-believe Stephen King character hovered over them, smiling and typing on the computer, then also disappeared.

A new light descended on the faces of Sidney and his friends.

"Get ready for another signpost in our quest," Sidney was carried away with his own enthusiasm.

23

"Hold hands in a circle again," Sidney said to his friends. "We`re going to sail away," his voice was ever so soothingly soft.

They held onto to each other`s hands tightly in a circle, and floated away through sunbeams, and suddenly, giant books appeared in the sky, flying around like birds, opening their pages. Sidney and his companions went through the words, sentences, paragraphs and chapters, they heard voices coming from the books. It was all fulfilling and untroubled.

Stephen King`s name was on the cover of all the books.

"What have you learnt so far?" Sidney asked his companions.

They breathed a great sigh of relief.

"In King`s novels and stories," Reavis said thoughtfully, "blood and power, power from deep inside every human being, that`s an important ingredient for success in any venture."

Stephanie cleared her throat then said, "There`s another thing at work in all or most of King`s work, the weak has power too, the disabled, the victim in society, all have tremendous potential and they have lessons to teach us all."

"That`s amazing!" Sidney embraced both Stephanie and Reavis.

"And I think all writers have a dark tower to which they strive," William said firmly, sunlight kissing his face. "It`s the supreme goal of every artist, not prizes. Also it`s self-discovery."

"Bravo! Bravo! William, that`s it!" Sidney was over jubilant, hugging and kissing him on the cheeks.

Then the four of them were hugging and kissing each other.

"We must use these lessons in our quest," Sidney`s voice rang like a bell. "As we saw in that hellish scene on the stage with the make-believe King; the real King still has the power to come through to us, that`s his deep power. All fiction must have that magical power. We are now over Colorado."

His companions looked puzzlingly at each other, "But weren`t we here before?" they asked together.

"Yes, but I`m feeling something we might have overlooked," Sidney`s eyes x-rayed the scene below them. "We`re all born with a light of seeing beyond our daily lives. It comes through prominently in some adults, and its strongest in child prodigies."

"Yes, yes," Stephanie said joyfully. "The boy in The Shining had it, yes, yes."

"I`m so happy that the three of you are so well enlightened now," Sidney smiled, his face bursting with inner sunshine. "That`s another clue, yes, The Shining."

"And buildings as well,"Reavis announced. "There`s the Marsten House, the haunted mansion in the Dark Tower, and, of course, this monstrosity below called, The Overlook Hotel."

"I`m sure King is imprisoned in some kind of a tomb-like place," Sidney was deep in thought. "Whether underground or over-ground, it`s some kind of a cocoon."

The Over-look Hotel in the novel, The Shining, materialised below them just as King had written it in the novel. Then a giant pen about the size of an aeroplane appeared and began to fly over their heads.

They were now dressed in denim jeans, shirts and sneakers. They heard voices chanting:

"King is the best storyteller in the world since Homer and Dickens! The Dark Tower is the finest work since the Odyssey!"

24

"Welcome to you four!" a voice seemed to come from the entire building.

Sidney felt a thrilling sensation in the pith of his stomach.

"Is that a character from The Shining novel?" asked Reavis, raising his voice a little.

"I don`t think so," Sidney replied, "remember, look inside and outside of King`s work. For King, the universe is a great story."

Could it be the five-year old boy, Danny, and will he help us? thought Stephanie.

William didn`t feel anything.

The front door opened and they descended, entering, Sidney leading, looking around at everything.

"That`s a supreme achievement!" the voice said and this time it seemed to come from above their heads.

They looked up.

"Stay focussed!" Sidney cautioned his companions.

"I am the voice of Dickens`s past!" the voice boomed, and it came from all around

"And I`m the voice of Homer`s past!" another voice sounded old, tired and breathless.

"It`s this building from the novel that is making all these noises," Reavis said as he spun around in the directions of the voices.

"Let youth speak!" Sidney commanded. "It has power!"

The building shook like it was in an earthquake.

"This is the voice of Tolstoy`s past!" another voice called out.

"Show yourselves, then!" Sidney demanded.

Then a child`s voice said shakily, "I`m here! You`ve come this far. Nothing can harm!"

"Speak for yourself, brat!" a voice raged. "I`m the voice of the Cyclops! Why have you wakened me from my ancient slumber!"

"I`m Nobody!" Sidney mocked with a cunning smile. "Remember me! My name is Nobody!"

"What! What! What are you doing here?" the voice asked sharply. "You are supposed to be sealed in another book!"

Sidney laughed and said, "I`m on a quest ! A quest to find another golden fleece!"

The voice thundered and shook the building, "I think you have lost your way!"

Sidney knew the jealous evil force was very clever in trying to get him to reveal his plans, so he shouted again, "My name is Nobody! I`m reading a children`s book and enjoying it! I`m searching for another children`s book!"

Now the building shook like it was in a terrible storm.

"Keep faith!" the child's voice, innocent and a little shaky spoke again. "Keep faith!"

Suddenly they were in an elevator going up and down crazily.

"What is it doing!" William's voice trembled but he wasn't frightened.

Maybe we're going to heaven and hell at the same time, Reavis thought.

"I am the voice of all the evil in all the stories that were ever written and yet to be written!" a voice thundered and shook the elevator violently. "Here you will get hungry and you will eat your own shit and be satisfied!"

They were now in a large room.

"What room number is this?" Stephanie asked, surveying the room.

"No, it's not Room 217," Sidney said calmly.

The room shook, then it began to get smaller and smaller. The four of them were huddled together like sardines in a small tin.

"Don't be afraid!" a voice spoke from the ceiling of the elevator. "Because, although the isle is full of noises, it has sweet airs and sweet sounds. I am the voice of the Bard I told you I will always be with you!"

The elevator began to resume its normal size.

"Thank you, Maestro!" Reavis called, looking upwards. "Are you going to stay with us here?"

The elevator began to get bigger and wider, filling with people wearing masks.

Outside a winter storm was closing in.

The elevator wrenched itself off from the building and rose skyward.

"What`s happening?" Reavis held onto Sidney`s shoulder. "I think the hotel is moving."

"Fasten your seat-belts, folks!" a deep voice blasted. "We`re going to hell!"

"Remember, I`m with you all the way!" the child`s voice chimed. "The Bard told me about your situation!"

The elevator was covered with snow, but as it went upwards, the snow began to melt, winds howled, the elevator began to descend, down and down it plunged like a downed aeroplane.

"Are we going to crash?" William shook.

The others wondered as well.

"Never! Never!" Sidney and the child`s voice said together.

Down and down the elevator plunged.

Stephanie and William held onto to each other. Reavis gripped Sidney`s shoulder. Sidney stood erect, firm and brave.

The elevator straightened and descended into what was a fiery furnace of leaping red and yellow flames like raging like hungry tongues eager for a taste of anything.

"Welcome to hell!" a voice thundered with sparks flying everywhere. "I Cancer, keeper of this damned hotel The winter storms cannot touch us down here! You four fuckers are doomed!"

"You can`t tempt us!" Sidney said calmly. "Go back to your blood and thunder."

"Blood and fire made your world!" the Cancer-keeper ranted and laughed. "Here! Take this!" And the Cancer-keeper materialised into a black dragon, snorting green flames at Sidney and his friends.

Sidney and his friends changed into a dog, cat, rabbit and a squirrel but kept their human brains and speech.

Sidney as the dog, barked, then said, "Take this!" and he and the others turned into every heroic character in every Stephen King's stories and novels; then they changed back into their former selves.

The elevator landed on top of a hill surrounded by gulping, boiling volcanic flames but the elevator wasn't damaged nor consumed. Blood began to surround the elevator. A woman's scream was heard. Then the wailing of babies.

"Help us! Help us!" children cried.

Sidney and his companions were calm and still unafraid.

Vampire bats flew into the elevator, circling over their heads.

"This time you won't get away!" a large black hairy bat with blood dripping mouth and red flaming eyes, spat and approached them.

"Be brave as always!" Sidney said to his companions, and they made a back-to-back circle and began to chant: "Let light shine! Shine! Shine!"

"Where is your fucking guides now, eh!" the bat snarled. "Burn! Burn, you and your kind.

Burn!"

"Let the man shine, shine, shine!" Sidney and his companions sang sweetly. "Let the children rejoice and shout! Power to the children!"

The vampire-bats began to dance around Sidney, spitting out, "Leader man, your blood has aids in it. You`re going to die!" And turning to Stephanie, spat out, "Don`t ever fuck with him again, woman! He`s going to kill you!"

"Shine! Shine! Shine! Little boy, shine!" Sidney and his companions chanted.

The bats growled, screamed, howled and grunted, flew around crazily then disappeared.

A woman and a boy appeared in the expanded elevator, the woman caressed the child`s head and said, "Son, why are you in the hell-hole. I`m sure one of these men is your father!"

She pushed the child away from her, suddenly angry with him.

"That`s not the child`s voice we`ve been hearing," Sidney said to his companions. "It`s another trick."

The elevator shook violently; there was a loud blast, then a great howl!

"Come away, oh infant child!" the woman`s voice wailed, now outside the elevator. "For the earth is dangerous and wild!"

A man`s drunken voice began to sing, "My mama she told me. Since I was a small child. A woman`s a three-face. A demon thing. That`s always going to bring .Blues in the wild!"

A disguised Sidney Prince suddenly appeared in the elevator, saying, "My name is Caretaker!" and walked around the real Sidney Prince and his companions, "Welcome to my hotel!

Come on, don`t you know! I`m Sidney Prince, your one and only faithful friend!"

"I`m here, you know that," the real Sidney Prince communicated to his companions.

"We`re in the book of real life. We`re in and out of story-books."

"What kind of shit is that woman!" the fake Sidney said to Stephanie. "I know you can shit bricks sweetly!"

And to Reavis, offered, "Here is some sparkling champagne and the best caviar! I bet you haven`t tasted such delicious food in your life?"

A small mahogany table appeared with a champagne-bucket with champagne and caviar.

"Come on, old fellow, you know you`d like it!" the fake Sidney Prince persisted.

Reavis and the others stared at the table but was unmoved, their stomachs were full.

"Don`t you want to toast your abilities so far?" the fake Sidney mocked cheerfully.

The elevator shook, swayed, tilted upside down but the real Sidney and his companions held their ground.

"You`re a bad actor!" Reavis shook his head and shouted at the fake Sidney.

"We`re all bad actors in this story, my dear fellow!" the fake Sidney bawled.

Reavis closed his eyes and concentrated deeply. The others joined him.

"Hold fast!" the real Sidney Prince said bravely.

They held fast.

The fake Sidney Prince changed into a huge green-eyed monster, shouting, "Gimme me damn talent, man! I wanna write it! One man shouldn`t have it all!"

The real Sidney and his companions were unaffected.

A child`s voice shouted, "Believe it! Believe all!"

The fake Sidney changed into a black hooded snarling, monster eating a baby.

The real Sidney closed his eyes and went into deep meditation with his companions.

In the expanded elevator, all around were bits of human flesh.

"Envy! Envy! Frustrated talents running wild!" a voice boomed. "I`m the everlasting bogey-man or woman of every jealous writer`s dream! Give me the flesh of the literary accomplishments!"

The elevator shook, screams were heard all around. Someone or something was banging away at a wall, door or partition with something like a sledgehammer.

"A giant boulder is going to smash Colorado!" the voice roared. "Remember me, I`m the Caretaker! Listen to me ! I`m going to kill that pen which isn`t working for me! Get away, you four pieces of rotten shits! You won`t get any literary light shining here! Who`s the imaginator!"

The voice of the child began to chant over their heads: "The imaginator gave me my special gift! Come with me, the blizzards are coming in!"

"What fucking blizzards!" the monster-voice boomed. "You`re in hot, imagined hell! Your father is inside and outside every sentence and paragraph of himself!"

The elevator turned upside down and right side up again.

"I have the power!" the child`s voice intoned. "I`m glowing ! Remember an entire world can exist in the tiniest grain of sand!"

There was an explosion! The elevator blew to bits. Screams were heard everywhere! But Sidney and his companions were safe and the heard the voice of child, saying reassuringly,

"All will be well! Have a safe journey!"

Sidney and his friends found themselves standing some yards away from a prison.

25

"Are we going inside that prison?" Reavis asked, his face sweating. "Is it necessary?"

Sidney smiled, his voice was sparkling, "Of course, Professor. "There`s something about this place I have to check out. It`s in the book, The Green Mile and outside the book. Something surrounding the area."

Reavis sighed deeply and looked at the others.

"Don`t you remember what the Bard said in his work," Stephanie said to him as he turned wide-eyed to face her, "That there are many things in heaven and earth that aren`t dreamt of in philosophy, something like that."

"Yes, of course, that`s from the play Hamlet," Reavis replied wearily.

"From here on, we`ll go through the most fearful, the most dangerous tests to prove our dedication to finding King," Sidney spoke with a hand on his heart.

The most amazing, the most fantastic transformation occurred, in front of the penitentiary, Reavis` eyes became red and bulging, his head swelled, his body blew up like a balloon, his eyes popped out of his head, his head and body split in halves, fell away and like a pregnant woman having a caesarean operation, giving birth to a middle-aged man, dripping blood, impeccably dressed in a grey suit, saying, "I`m a publisher! Where`s the finished book, Prince? It has been a long journey. Let me see and read this new story?"

Sidney laughed and embraced the publisher who was tall, handsome, greying at the temples, black shining shoes, white shirt and Eton-tie.

Stephanie and William enjoyed the moment.

The Publisher changed into a giant black man scantily clad and barefooted.

Stephanie began touching herself all over, saying, "I feel so nice and yet not so nice!" she was smiling all over, then her body began to shake, swell, her eyes popped out of her head and flew around Sidney, staring questioningly at him.

"Don`t waver, keep strong!" Sidney said, still smiling widely.

Stephanie`s body burst!

Sidney was still smiling.

William began to shake, spin like a top, then jumped up and down and split into two halves from his head to his navel.

"This is going to be a great novel!" said the giant black man, gathering the various parts of the bodies of Sidney and his companions, held them up to the sky in his enormous hands, his huge mouth opened whispering something the mind of Sidney couldn`t understand. The prison doors opened, and, Sidney coming together in all his body, followed the giant black man/publisher inside the prison. "My friends have disintegrated into the wonders of the imagination," he muttered.

They entered a room with an electric-chair, the giant black man/publisher placed the body parts of Sidney's companions on the large electric-chair, they fitted perfectly on the chair, then in a commanding voice, "Come to life with more strength again!" the power was turned on, and after an hour in which there were swoons, laments and singing, Reavis, Stephanie and William, stood before Sidney, smiling. The giant black man/publisher disappeared. On the floor was a book with Stephen King's name on it. Sidney picked it up excitedly, but When he opened the book, the pages were blank.

"Get out of here!" Some prison-guards called to them and ushered them out.

And the great prison disappeared.

Sun shone on their faces, their bodies glowing brightest. The sky was cloudless.

"Let's go into this nest of vipers!" Sidney said cheerfully and moved forward with his friends following.

Faraway they heard a great sound which seemed like thunder: a human voice blasting against the sky, angry at unfavourable elements. Then real thunder roared, then lightning forked and rain poured like a flooded river.

They sailed over a great mountain, passed through cities, towns, villages and vast countrysides, not knowing where they were. Sometimes the sun shone the brightest they ever saw, and sometimes snow fell, whitening landscapes. But on and on they kept going.

Sometimes they saw Stephen King being chased by a large rabid dog, other times King was being bitten by a vampire bat, and in another scene, King was getting thinner and thinner and thinner until he became invisible.

Sidney and his companions were refreshed by a scene in which John Smith of the Dead Zone, was hanging on a cross, shrouded in white in sky above clouds, saying, "In King`s house there are many mansions! There`s a place for all four of you!"

The triumph of the innocents, Sidney thought and his companions heard his voice in their hearts.

26

"We`ve learnt a lot from that experience, I`m sure," Sidney said as they now walked on the ground somewhere in America.

His companions looked at each other. Stephanie was the first to speak, "Well, Coffey was a Christ-like figure."

"Coffey had a tremendous amount of humility," Reavis beamed.

"And like Christ, he conquered death by dying on the in the electric-chair, a cross-symbol,"

William`s face shone sun-like as he spoke.

"Yes, Bill, he escaped," Sidney smiled. "They couldn`t hold his miraculous being."

They were all smiling and happy.

"I`ve also found this is the penitentiary," Sidney held up a cartridge- fountain pen in front of them. "After his accident in 1999, King was in terrible pain for six months and to ease the pain he wrote with this pen."

"My God, that`s indeed magic!" Reavis` eyes flashed.

Stephanie and William had the same experience.

"Remember anything is possible is a King`s story," Sidney went on. "And we`re about to meet the pandemic plague!"

"We`re strong!" his companions said together.

The surroundings were suddenly gloomy, trees and buildings were black, dark clouds rolled by, and there were dead bodies everywhere. The stench seemed to wiped out the animal life.

"I`m even ready for death and beyond," Sidney said bravely.

"We`re prepared!" his companions answered.

"If they`re holding King in the worse hell, we`ll find and rescue him," Sidney said, looking around at over-turned cars, trucks, vans and other vehicles; then he saw a daffodil growing blooming near a blackened oak.

The air became foggy and black with soot which encircled them. They began to smell the rotten carnage. They held their nerve and managed to ward off any discomfort.

"Always keep faith!" Sidney yelled, his voice rang through the desolate scene. "We`re going to meet the Great Queen. She`ll take us from this plague-ridden place!"

A voice laughed and laughed mockingly, then said, "What can save you now, searchers! You`re doomed in my gloom! Give it up the chase! I`m going to crush the four spider-fuckers!"

Sidney took out the cartridge-pen and waved it about, and they could see a clear path in front of them and a spotlight shining on a building, they followed the clear patch and saw a huge figure of a woman sitting in front of the building, she was African-American about twenty feet tall, naked with her legs tightly closed.

"Mother! Mother! There you are!" Sidney shouted, running to her with his companions following. "Oh, loving mama, give us sanctuary!" Then he touched the huge black legs with the cartridge-pen and they opened wide, wider, until the lips of her huge vagina opened like an succulent mouth.

"Come on! Come on, quickly!" Sidney said to his companions. "We`re been severely tested here!"

His companions followed very quickly, panting.

Sidney touched the great lips of the giant black queen`s vagina and he and his companions entered and the great lips closed tightly again.

Inside the great vagina, they entered her great womb of blue sky, sun shining, trees green, birds singing and buildings stood erect and inviting.

"She must be related to John Coffey?" Reavis speculated, looking up at the amazing sky.

"In a way, yes," said Sidney.

"Did you notice that building outside is a library?" Stephanie said to them.

"Yes, I saw that," Sidney replied.

William and Stephanie nodded.

"Another clue, the library, yes," Sidney went on. "We`re very safe. The queen will deliver us from anything or anyone trying to hinder us."

The scene changed again and they were in the library, but the library had no shelves of books. They heard singing, loud blues singing from outside the library.

"The queen, the mother of all is singing," Sidney was smiling filled with rainbow colours.

Suddenly, the library began to fill up with shelves of books and every book had Stephen King`s face and name on it. Voices from the books joined in the blues singing.

Sidney recognised the voices as he said, "All the main characters in King`s books are singing." And he began to dance around his three companions whose faces became moon-radiant as they danced with him.

"We shall survive anything! Bring it on!" Sidney`s voice echoes around the library.

They saw the characters of the novel, The Stand who had survived the plague in the story, coming towards them, waving and smiling and joining in the singing and dancing.

"Hurrah! For the King!" they all chanted.

"The supreme jealous one is hot on your trail!" the giant black queen stopped singing and warned Sidney and his friends.

"Thank you, Mama. I know the line between the worlds are becoming thinner. But we know that in the imagination of King everything is possible." Sidney breathed deeply and felt a new bloom in his heart.

"Well said, my son!" the queen sang and her voice echoed through his entire being.

"You`re an amazing reader. You`re not just constant reader nor a ardent fan. You go beyond words. The power of the imagination opens up and explode into worlds beyond life and death."

Sidney felt that he was the only one who could hear her voice.

Then Nick Andros stepped forward into a shining spotlight, he too was shining with a handsome face and very healthy-looking and he could detect all the instincts of creation, hear, smell, speak in new languages with keen sense of meaning. "I can hear the whisper of fly", he beamed at Sidney. "Always remember the jealous critics move from story to story, book to book. Creation is better than destruction! Beware of glittering prizes!"

There was a boom above their heads as the ceiling of library blasted open and a darkening sky revealed a black scaly demon with fiery red eyes, red tongue, claws like a large tiger which growled at them, "It`s not over yet! You lucky survivors!" The eyes of the beast burned everything except Sidney and his friends. "Pestilence shall be your destiny!" it bellowed.

"Stand firm and strong! The queen`s voice sang. "We`re on the right hand of King! He`s writing in your very souls and showing you where he is!"

The black demon flew over the roofless library, snorted fire, smashed trees and pounded ground with its great tail and clenched claws-fists.

A few survivors of the plague disappeared.

A giant copy of The Stand novel opened and flapped like wings then also disappeared.

"In the tongue and name of King I speak!" the queen`s voice rang out. "Demon subjects like you are always vanquished! King is the knight with pen-sword who destroys demons!"

The black demon laughed, grunted, "Remember, King created me too!"

"What has been created can be destroyed or certainly controlled!" Sidney said. "The writers in King`s stories are coming to finish you off!"

"King`s life is with us!" the queen sang.

"How are you going to escape me this time!" the demon roared and blue and red fire flew from its mouth. "I have every fatal disease in my stomach!" Its stench was beginning to creep into the nostrils of Sidney and his companions.

The demon changed from black to white, then to red, then to yellow, flames streaming from its nostrils, mouth, eyes and pointed ears.

"Hold on, sweet Prince!" the queen sang and began to hum the sweetest sound Sidney and his friends ever heard, the sound surrounded their souls and they joined in the humming.

"From every accident comes strength!" the queen chimed. "From every disaster comes creativity!"

Sidney and his companions hummed.

"Stop this shit!" the demon blasted. "I`m going to get him this time! This time he`s going to be lost forever!"

The humming went on sweetly and steadily.

"What the fuck is all this about!" the demon stormed on. "I have dynamite in my stomach. I`ll blow you and your books to pieces!" It stamped its feet, breathed fire of every colour and howled, and from its mouth came white flies, flying around, buzzing loudly.

"Keep the music in your soul, children!" the queen cautioned.

Stephanie`s stomach began to rumble, swell, she looked at it, rubbed it, something was moving inside her, she rubbed violently, her eyes popping, then her stomach swelled and swelled and burst! Bumble bees came out and began chasing and eating the white flies.

Sidney, Reavis and William stared in wonderment.

"Hum, children, hum sweetly!" the queen persisted. "Keep it up and strong!"

They heeded her, even Stephanie whose stomach now began to close and return to normalcy.

The library disappeared and now they were in a wide field covered with red roses, and the giant black queen was sitting on a mahogany chair in the field, humming. The sun blazed down. The queen`s merry face was all smiles as she said, "Sweet Prince, you`re going to find him! All epics lead to his trail! He has given you an insight into his imagination. Use it well. You`re a reading genius. Keep on humming, my children!" She stood up, erect, smiling.

Then demon snorted, farted and jumped in the air. "I`ll take this place off the map!" And now clouds of white flies appeared again all around the field of red roses, they outnumbered the bees who now seemed to be retreating. The thickness of the cloud of white flies began to block out the sunlight.

The queen let out a great groan. Sidney sneezed, Stephanie belched, Reavis and William farted loudly together. And all the red roses turned to sun-flowers letting off a white dust which killed off all the white flies.

Sidney felt an electric thrill running through his body.

The demon laughed and laughed, "Fuck Lovecraft! Fuck Harlan Ellison!" It boomed, snarled, blew fire and flew around the field. "I`m not finished! Never! This isn`t the last of me! I`m going to devour all the books in the world! I`m going to swallow the sun and moon of all creative imagination!"

The queen became white, red, yellow and then black again. She opened her great thighs and blood came out from her great vagina, first, a trickle, then a flood, and the flood of blood began to change into a huge Stephen King standing about twelve feet tall and holding a portable typewriter in one huge hand, his eyes fixed on the demon.

"Where are you, Mr King?" Sidney asked telepathically.

"Not yet, and certainly not here," was the reply.

Sidney was the only one who heard these words.

The giant Stephen King began to type, his fingers moved magically.

The demon fell over and began to have fits and spasms. "Where`s the dynamite! Where`s the sword of destruction!" it bawled in anguish.

Stephanie, Reavis and William felt their bodies throbbing with ecstasy. Stephanie was whole again.

"Get to fuck away from here, vampire!" Sidney shouted at the now groaning demon lying in the field.

Sunshine and blue skies brightened their faces, the queen was humming; Reavis, Stephanie and William were hugging each other, then everything faded, and Sidney and his companions were the only ones standing in the field of sun-flowers, radiant sunshine and the bluest sky.

Birds sang an enchanting melody, and not far away, a brook gurgled sweetly. Then sunrays haloed their heads, brighter than stars.

27

Now Sidney and his companions were standing outside the home of King in Bangor, Maine.

"Should we go in?" asked Reavis, his voice heavy.

Sidney took a long while before he responded, "I`m not quite sure we should. Because I don`t think we`re ready yet. And we cannot expose his family or friends to any danger."

A raven flew over their heads, squawked and disappeared.

"Well," Reavis went on, tapping Sidney`s shoulder, "what now?"

There was a scream for help which came from deep inside the house. "Hurry! Hurry!

Don`t give up the fight!" the scream articulated. Then lots of pages from books began to come out of opening windows. There were noises of typewriters/word-processors coming out as well. "Find the page of a castle," a whisper came into Sidney`s ear, he ran and grabbed at the flying pages, examining each one, his eyes popped as he found the page with the word, "castle" on it, he smiled and breathed deeply.

Meanwhile his companions were also running after pages and examining them.

"It's all right! I've found it!" Sidney communicated to them. "In the most savage hell, there's always hope. In the deepest heart of darkness, a bright light shines! King is held in a castle somewhere. I don't know yet. We're nearing the place. CASTLE! CASTLE! Remember that word. We'll astound all the evil jealous critics."

Sun-flowers began to rain down on them. The sun smiled widely, and in the deep recesses of their minds, they saw King reunited happily with his family and friends.

Sidney and his companions felt evermore stronger, their hearts leaping skyward.

Suddenly they were in an underground cave lit by torches.

"Here again," Sidney muttered, "what's the matter?"

"Hell fiction, my young foe!" A voice boomed all around the underground. "I've a load of dynamite to excite and destroy you! Here are my children! Come out of the unsettled jealous dark stories!"

Huge spiders with word-processors on them appeared, crawling around the cave, their eyes bright and searching.

"How do you like them! They're beautiful, aren't they!" the voice howled. "Get them, my children, web them!" And a great grey web fell on Sidney and his companions. The spiders were making sucking and clicking sounds.

Once again thunder struck as if the known world had exploded. The entire underground shook, swayed, turned upside down, spun and righted.

"Fire! Burn the books!" the voice raged and whirled all around. "You're doomed, readers!

Get ready to be finished!"

Sidney touched the web with the cartridge-pen, and he and his companions were now inside a giant egg.

"Where are you!" the voice blasted. "Clever at hiding, eh!"

Inside the giant egg, Sidney and his friends saw a large mirror, they looked deeply into it, and saw the face of King, the egg began to crack, to hatch!

"Where the fuck are they!" the voice snarled.

The voice couldn`t see nor detect the giant egg.

When the giant egg cracked open, Sidney and his companions were in a busy street. It was Spring. They thought they saw J.K .Rowling coming towards them, pointing at something, they couldn`t make it out. The city seemed to be silent, people were going about their business quietly.

We`re in the best of hands, Sidney thought and smiled.

Their appetites were satisfied and their thirst was quenched.

"When a writer has a readership as great as King`s and as deep and penetrating as this Prince fellow, that writer is worth more than any Nobel Prize!"

Sidney and his companions heard these words in their minds.

"They can capture his body," Sidney muttered, "but they can never capture his imagination."

The sun cuddle their faces.

"The evil spawn is out to destroy the creation of all books," Sidney said, his voice echoing all around. "But in King all evil criticism will be defeated!"

Stephanie felt Sidney`s voice penetrating her sexual centre, she was becoming overwhelmingly attracted to him, she trembled with ecstasy.

"Maybe King wasn`t kidnapped," Sidney said thoughtfully.

His companions stared at him, amazed.

"Well, remember with Stephen King anything is possible," he smiled.

"I mean, it could be a creative, experimental thing. A writer like King, lives in his imagination most of the time."

Now they looked at him mysteriously, their hearts and minds racing.

A clown suddenly appeared, laughing and pushing a wheel-barrow overflowing with books.

"You haven`t seen this!" the clown snapped and lit a match. "If you say King is in every book, I`m going to burn these books! I`ve all his books in this wheel-barrow!" the clown held up the lighted match which now looked like a torch and snarled at Sidney and his companions, "What do you say about that, eh!"

Sidney laughed, "King can go in and out!"

"All writers can!" the clown jeered.

"Not like the King!" Sidney said triumphantly. "You`ve kidnapped his body, that`s all. The ransom you desire, you can never have. Your tricks won`t work. Where`s he?"

"I want the soul of his imagination!" the clown screamed, "otherwise I`ll burn these precious books! Give me his mind!"

The clown blew out the lighted match, looking puzzled. "I`m not going to fucking tell you where his body is. You four pieces of rotten shits! I`ve read all King`s books and stories!"

"But you can`t read like his true fans!" Sidney laughed again. "And if you burn the books, you`ll destroy yourself as well!"

Sidney`s companions joined in his laughter.

"What! Yes! No! You`ve tricked me!" the clown raged and disappeared in a puff of blue smoke with his wheelbarrow of books. "You haven`t seen the last of us! I`ll be in your dreams as well!" its voice trailed off in the distance.

The sun glowed orange in a bright blue sky as Sidney and his companions set off.

Although the sky was bright and welcoming, the inhabitants of the city looked tired, haunted and frightened. They stared in the direction of Sidney and his friends but didn`t see them.

"I`m so glad we`re invisible to people," Reavis reflected, eyeing the silent surroundings.

"We understand that as well," Stephanie and William said together.

Stephanie felt all the love in all possible worlds growing inside her, she felt she was inside Sidney and he was inside her.

"Yes, he`s wonderful, I know," William whispered in her ear.

They smiled and Reavis also smiled.

At night the moon and stars accompanied them. In the day-time, sometimes the sun shielded, caressed and smiled at them, at other times, thunder. lightning, rain, snow, sleet and hurricane-winds chased them. But they went on, relentlessly, unharmed, defiant and stronger.

They were walking along near a forest, when a middle-aged man dressed in a black suit wearing dark glasses, limping with a walking-stick, approached them. He seemed to touch them with his presence, his voice seemed to echo as he spoke, introducing himself, "Hello, good day to you all! I`m Richard Bachman!"

"That`s the pen-name of King!" Sidney and his companions exclaimed.

I`ll take you to where they`re hiding him! They want a King`s ransom for his release!" Then the Bachman-character began to laugh loudly, then said, "I like that pun, a King`s ransom for the release of Stephen King!"

There was a pause, then the Richard Bachman sighed heavily and said, "Come, follow me!

"Are you sure, you`re Bachman?" Sidney probed, his eyes seeming to cut through the Bachman-character`s body.

"I am he! I am! That is a pure fact! Tell everybody!" the Bachman-character shouted. "Tell it to the heavens! I am I am Bachman! Tell the whole world!"

"Why are you here?" Reavis cut in.

"Whose disappearance are you seeking?"

"My dear fellow, how kind of you to ask," the Bachman character swayed, his voice swayed with his body. "I should ask you the same question. Why are you really here, eh?

"What is going on here, Sid?" Reavis turned to face Sidney.

"It`s a secret!" the Bachman –character chuckled. "The stupid clown didn`t know it. I`m keeping a watchful eye on King. Nothing bad is going to touch him. After all, he`s my other half. My better half."

The sky suddenly darkened. Thunder boomed! High winds began and to sweep everything with a hurricane force, uprooting trees, tearing up the earth and roofs off buildings, over-turning vehicles and blowing people through the air like bits of paper. Now screams, howls, moans, wails, groans were heard, then laughter.

"Here it comes again! I must be off!" said the Bachman character. "But I`m with you in every word and sentence and chapter. I hide sometimes because some people can`t read properly. They don`t know the difference between a book and its cover." And the Bachman disappeared.

"I`m going to eat the four of you!" a voice bawled out.

Then a little man about two feet tall appeared, dressed in a purple suit, bow-tie, white shirt and shining brown shoes. His eyes, green, his hair black and greying at the sides. "Please to make your acquaintance!" he smiled and the smile was the width of his round youngish face. "I`m sorry, I didn`t recognise the four of you at first. Everything is a mess, isn`t it. But I`m sure you and I can fix things!"

"Where are your toys?" Sidney asked with a cunning look. "Have you forgotten to bring them as presents for us?" Sidney laughed loudly and pointed at the little man`s head which began to burst open and packets wrapped in Christmas-paper, began coming out of the bursting head.

"Oh, the pen-name, the pen-name! You`ve met the pen-name!" the now twisting mouth of the little man cried out. "You too are losers! You belong to the club! Next time I`ll get you through the word-processor!" and he disappeared.

Sidney and his companions hurried off. The sky was bright again. They heard a soft voice Whispering in their ears, "Edwin! Edwin!"

"That`s King`s middle name!" Sidney exclaimed happily. "In a story, place and time do not necessarily mean what they mean in real life. The most important thing is that we find the clue, the key to unlock King`s prison and free him."

"What a treasure!" Stephanie`s heart leapt in her throat.

"Simply divine, I say," Reavis beamed.

William was enchanted.

They were now in a red convertible –car, driving along the Champs Elysees, then near to Hyde Park, London, then near the Coliseum in Rome: people were smiling and waving at them. They waved back happily.

"Our destiny is near," Sidney said, his heart beating fast.

The others shared his enthusiasm.

In Athens, they saw the ghost of Homer being chased by a giant spider with the head of a snarling dog. The ghost of Homer tossed them a book, Sidney caught it and when he opened it, the face of King was on every page, smiling and saying, "You`re on the last stage of your journey! Come on, my saviours!"

Reavis felt his skin peeling off his body which grew hot and cold at the same time.

Stephanie felt fingers caressing her body gently, it was her sweetest pleasure, she closed her eyes for a moment, enjoying herself. William`s head throbbed with excitement and wonder.

Sidney felt totally fulfilled, in touch with everything.

Golden sunbeams sparkled their faces. The air was the sweetest perfume. Trees were whispering to them, birds, bees and butterflies flew around in haloes around buildings and hills and mountains. They were floating through the air once again. The car disappeared from beneath them. They were travelling through time and out of time in the wonders of space.

They realised a new interpretation of the world of creative literature. They drifted away and a new sun went with them.

Now they were sailing over Africa, then over Asia, then over Arabia. They hovered over every country for a long while, searching for any clue, signal or signpost.

28

Over South America, they saw fires, bush-fires burning away the jungles. A multi-coloured bird flew over the flames with something in its beak, when it came near to Sidney and his friends they saw it was a pair of spectacles. The bird flew above them and dropped the spectacles in Sidney`s lap and flew off.

"Yes! Yes!" Stephanie said jubilantly, her face lit up like a Christmas tree. "I see it. Stephen King wears spectacles. Yes! Another clue and signpost!"

"Yes, Sid!" Reavis and William said together. "Clever!"

"That`s it, yes!" Sidney was enchanted. "Now let`s go!"

They flew off like they were on a magic carpet.

A booming voice from the flames called after them, "This is hell! I start fires on every page! I`ll get you in the hottest pursuit! Fires scream! Explosion screaming and coming after you from hell!"

Sidney laughed and said, "Laughter cures all! It`s all a divine comedy!"

"I think in every story, King is re-creating the world," Reavis` voice was cool, calm and collected.

"Wise words, my friend," William said gently.

Sidney put the spectacles on and smiled at his companions. "We`ve gathered a lot from our journey. As we`re coming to the end of our quest. I must warn you again that this is going to be the most dangerous part of the quest. If any of you want to get out of it, now is the time to say so. I`ll understand. I`m in a life and death struggle."

"We`re with you all the way", they communicated to Sidney from the depths of their souls.

They held hands together, formed a circle and went into deep meditation for a long while.

"Beyond the forbidden rivers and seas, we shall ride the waves to eternity! And we shall destroy all the jealous critics once and for all!" Sidney`s voice echoed through their minds and bodies.

A giant hand, wielding a giant feather-pen, drew a circle around the four. "You are protected," it wrote in the sky.

They were exceedingly satisfied.

"Your words are in your deeds in the imagination of King," the giant feather-pen wrote.

"Then on we go!" Sidney sang.

"So it is written so it shall be done!" the feather-pen wrote and waved goodbye.

Sidney and his companions flew through the sunlit air. They sailed away beyond hours, days, weeks, months and years. They were in other dimensions in the imagination of King.

As they approached a town, they couldn`t tell where, they heard a great crash, like a vehicle in an accident and someone groaning, "Help me! Help me, please!"

"That sounds familiar," Stephanie said, touching Sidney`s senses.

"Yes, it does," Sidney said calmly. "We have keys to open doors of strange kingdoms."

The sky was radiant.

"Whoever is in that accident is going to be all right," Sidney breathed deeply.

They saw a limping man walking on the side-walk, first, slowly, then quickly, then he began to run, finally jumping up in the air and laughing, "I`m feeling great! Now I don`t need a walking-stick anymore! I can write the greatest story of my life!" and he disappeared.

Suddenly, the ground heaved, bubbled and burst open like an earthquake exploding: there were cracks everywhere. Underground pipes burst, overflowing the streets and long thin figures dressed in black velvet shrouds began to emerge from the cracks in the ground.

"We`re going to fuck and eat every woman in this place!" one of the long thin figures shouted. "Fuck and eat every woman on this illiterate planet!"

"You`re not going to win!" Reavis thought.

The others agreed and Sidney shouted, "No, you`re not going to win!"

"Who the hell are you!" the long thin figure bawled, its eyes crimson and glittering.

"I`m a very deep reader, that`s all I`m going to tell you!" Sidney said calmly.

"Get out of our way!" Reavis` voice was very angry.

"No way, foolish one!" the long thin figure shrieked. "I want the woman!"

The surroundings became dark with what looked like a moon hiding in dark clouds.

Then lights were moving in the sky at an incredible speed, joining and separating, darting this way and that.

"It`s night! I didn`t see the change," William muttered, his eyes searching the scene.

"You must be reading a strange story, young fellow!" the long thin figure snapped.

"Here we go!"

Blood began to rain down on Sidney and his companions.

William felt queasy, his stomach heaved, ached and swelled.

Stephanie`s stomach also heaved, ached and swelled.

Reavis` head began to swell and ache.

"Oh, God, they`re inside us!" Stephanie, Reavis and William cried, swaying, staggering about.

They were now on the ground. The heaving and splitting of the earth ceased.

Sidney came between them and hugged, steadied and comforted them.

A large, round disc, a space-ship with lights all around the sides hovered over them, letting off a humming sound.

"Speak, brave one, speak!" a voice wavering, called from the space-ship.

Stephanie, Reavis and William pulled away from Sidney`s embrace, looking up at the space-ship, holding out their arms, eyes unblinking and said together, "Tell us what to do!

We`re bound to hear and understand!" and they turned quickly, stared at Sidney, snarled and blew fire from their mouths. "Taste the fire from another world, brave one! You`ll be like all the rest! Poison splitting you wide open!"

A car screeched around a corner suddenly and headed towards them. Shakespeare was in the driving-seat, laughing.

"Somehow I knew it would be the Bard!" Sidney beamed and pointed.

Shakespeare drove the, a blue ford-sedan towards Stephanie, Reavis and William, knocking them over. There were howls of pain as the three lay whimpering on the side-walk.

Shakespeare got out of the car and the car disappeared and he held Sidney`s hand tightly and together they shouted at the three lying on the side-walk, "Get out! Get out! You don`t belong in this scene! Out! Out! You are a brief candle!"

The figures of Stephanie, Reavis and William cringed, spat blood, wriggled, moaned and groaned in utter pain.

"Come out! Come out! We are a strong team against you!" Shakespeare and Sidney chanted, their voices steady and strong. "We will keep this bond forever in all the words of King!"

"Get up!" Shakespeare said to the three companions lying on the side-walk. "Keep the faith!"

"Yes, yes, take us!" the three answered, sobbing. "That was a difficult test. We`re true."

They rose up, dusted themselves as if nothing had happened, smiling, their faces glowing golden.

"Oh, brave ones! You are truly worthy of Stephen King works!" a voice circled overhead.

"I`ve gone inside them, trying to take them over. But they are too strong and true. They are all powerful!"

Suddenly, the sky was grey and all around was covered with a grey mist.

Stephanie took off all her clothes and was completely naked, then she half-stooped, opened her legs and blood began to pour out of her vagina, the blood flooded out, her eyes flashed red piercing lights. The grey sky and surrounding grey mist began to disappear. Then a whining, anguish, a sorrowful cry as the space-craft streamed away into the sky and into deep space. All the grey gloom was lifted.

Stephanie stood up erect, satisfied with herself.

"We`re getting more and more formidable," Sidney said as Shakespeare patted him on the shoulder.

"In your company everything is possible," Shakespeare said, surveying the four companions.

"But you must still travel in secret."

"We understand," they said.

"Search the world. It is becoming smaller," Shakespeare said. "Everything is created with

The lightning of the imagination. The quest is coming to an end. Remember, when you read my work, there I am also. The same with Stephen King." And the Bard vanished.

29

Surrounding hills green and rustling with cool fresh breezes; bird-songs echoing sweet and the new sun shone into their breasts. Indeed, the place where King was held was near, they felt it.

"Like Ulysses, we`ve already journeyed beyond ourselves," Sidney said with a fulfilled voice.

"We`ll never be the same again. We`ve caught every dream of King."

"Oh, King, here we come!" Stephanie, Reavis and William chanted.

Now blazing red roses fell on and all around them, and the bluest sky opened up and showed other earth-like planets and other home-like galaxies.

"Sidney loves!" Stephanie swooned.

Now they were floating enchantingly on the sparkling red roses, and every book of King was floating along with them.

Faraway, they heard a voice calling: "Come! Hurry! Come on!" It was a middle-aged man`s voice, happy and impatient.

And from every street, vehicles with voices from their horns and engines, cheered Sidney and his companions on.

"Even the machines are on our side," Reavis said happily.

"From now on they too will make new sounds," Sidney said cheerfully.

"The van that struck King in the accident will weep," William said. "And that`s another clue and key."

"Yes, yes," Stephanie said hurriedly.

"In the future cars will make themselves and have more control," Sidney said philosophically. "I read it everywhere."

They were floating along on a ray of golden sunshine with the books accompanying them.

"Every car has a story to tell," Sidney stared down at the streets with their busy traffic.

A horn from a car blared louder than all the others, and Sidney and his friends understood what that meant.

"Everything is connecting wonderfully," Sidney said, his face emitting rays of blue lights.

A large Alsatian dog appeared, wagging its tail, then snapping at them.

Sidney raised a hand with the cartridge-pen and the dog disappeared.

They felt a great buzzing in their bodies, looked at each other.

A giant computer-screen appeared above them showing King captive surrounded by a black metal ring.

"We`re coming!" Sidney shouted at the computer-screen. "For King and Story!"

"King! King! King!" his companions chanted.

"We`re living the reality of fiction," Reavis breathed.

"Stephen King has saved fiction," Stephanie said, lit up in smiles.

They heard the ticking of a clock.

"The great clock of time is showing us the way!" Sidney said, his voice deep, loud and echoing.

On and on they went, now in the deepest reaches underground, through cities, towns, villages, forests, jungles, seen and unseen, darkness and light, summer, winter, Spring and Autumn and again through the deep reaches underground.

The books and the giant computer-screen all disappeared. Now they were silent for most and remainder of the journey.

30

"Now we`re descending into hell-like scenes, my friends!" Sidney called out. "The city of sorrows, if you like."

The surroundings were red with blood and fire, groans moans and weeping were heard. But through cracks and crevices and apertures, the outside modern world crept in: mobile-phones, computers, the Web, Satellite-dishes, videos, television, CD, DVD, all were discernible.

They heard grunting, howling and snarling; they saw a giantess drinking and urinating blood, and a giant with horns eating babies from a huge dish. Then a dragon appeared, laughing and snorting fire, "Welcome!" It blasted at the four. "Ugliness is Beauty!" it went on and disappeared.

"Keep the faith," Sidney said to his companions telepathically. "Keep strong." And they nodded.

"Come on, seekers!" a voice called out. "Your world is going to end with a fucking bang and a whimper!"

They heard gunfire, explosions and more weeping.

"We`re going through the email:" "evil.uncreative.dot. com."" Sidney said, his voice ominous.

His companions felt all his emotions.

"We`re going to win," Reavis chimed.

"That`s our true spirit," Stephanie and William said.

"Read! Read! Read!" the four chanted.

"It has been the longest walk of literary life," Sidney said, his voice now soothing.

Then a word-processor went past them calling out: "Hurry! Save me! The word within all words, read between the lines!"

"Location! Location! Show yourself!" Sidney called out.

Everything went black. A voice screamed: "Turn back! Turn back! Before it`s too late!"

"Pay no attention to that!" Sidney cautioned his companions. "All the imaginations of the great writers, living and dead are with us! Come along, fear not!"

They were hot on the scent of Stephen King.

This has been the longest read of my life, Reavis thought.

The plot gets thicker and thicker, Stephanie thought.

William nodded.

Their ear-bells began to ring almost deafeningly.

All writers have to go through some dreadful kind of suffering, Sidney thought.

But blood is thicker than pain, William thought.

All roads lead to a dark tower, Sidney thought.

Now their bodies were shaking violently.

They held each other`s hand tightly and breathed deeply.

Our minds are very strong and faithful, Sidney thought.

Voices began to call: "I`m Stephen King! I`m Stephen King! Listen to me! Read this! I`m

King!"

"Pay no attention to those voices", Sidney communicated to his friends.

Their stomachs rumbled, growled and whispered, " I`m hungry! Feed King!"

They paid no attention to the voices.

Rotten smells assailed their nostrils like the stench of rotting corpses. They took deep breaths and blocked out the foul stench.

The heard a woman`s voice, crying and saying, "I`m Mrs King! Mr. Prince! Why are you trying to kidnap my son! Leave him alone!"

On and on Sidney and his companions went, ignoring and blocking out foul scents and cries.

A voice boomed, "Fuck you! Fuck you! Fuck the pages you`re written on! You four pieces of rotten corpses. Where is the missing page!"

"We seek the Castle, that`s where Stephen King is being held," Sidney communicated to his friends.

31

In the far distance, they heard the clicking of type-writers and word-processors. Then a solemn sun peered through dark clouds and spotlighted a castle. Knives, daggers, poisoned arrows came at them, but Sidney said, "Think of Carrie and all will be well."

They did so and all were safe. The knives, daggers, poisoned arrows bumped off their bodies.

"Carrying on with your wonderful story, Stephen!" Sidney called at the top of his voice.

His companions inhaled all his words.

"That is the meaning of words!" Shakespeare spoke in their minds.

King spoke to them in their imagination: "In my world of fiction, Beethoven can hear; Ray Charles and John Milton can see. Mozart, Keats and Charlie Parker didn`t die young and Van Gogh has both ears."

On and on they journeyed towards the castle. Now they were out of the hell-like scene were walking briskly. People saw them and smiled and waved at them. They smiled and waved back.

Sunshine smiled brightly on their faces.

"All together, Castle! Castle! Castle! Here we come!" Sidney chanted with the others joining in, their faces glistening with great joy.

A great door of happiness was opening.

"King! King! King!" they called out, their voices echoing all around.

"Come home! Come home!" a voice rang through their hearts.

All the books and stories written by Stephen King appeared again, floating in the air around them and came along with them which only they could see.

The castle was perched majestically on a hill with dark clouds hovering over the scene.

"King is very much alive," Sidney said, his tone melodious.

This jealous evil thing or things that kidnapped King must be preventing him from winning the Nobel Prize, Reavis thought.

The others felt the sentiment.

"Very true, my friend," Sidney responded to Reavis.

They began to climb the hill.

"We`re ready," Reavis, Stephanie and William said.

"The ink and blood of King`s everlasting pen will guide us," Sidney sang, leading them up the hill.

On top of the hill the castle glowed with orange, blue and red lights.

The worse thing a reader or critic can do to a writer is to tell him or her what and how to write, Sidney thought.

His friends nodded.

The world seemed to shake but the sunshine held its own.

Sidney and his companions steeled themselves.

"I`m a deep, deep reader!" Sidney shouted, his voice had a strange quality as it bounced off the sky.

"Our reading-eyes follow you!" his companions chanted, their faces shining with dazzling colours.

"All the creative talents in this world and the next defend us in the name of Stephen King!" Sidney was prayer-like.

Now they heard bells ringing and singing.

The castle shook a little.

"King has uncovered the secrets of literary life and death," Sidney said.

"Blood and life of the pen," his companions said.

"Stephen, we`re here! You`re free!" Sidney called out his voice echoing all over the castle.

32

The castle now spun like a top. Sun blazed. The castle stopped spinning and began to shine golden, brightening the surroundings.

Sidney felt like a knight of old; he lifted himself like a helicopter, hovering, then flew upwards, then circling the top of the castle. He felt a buzzing in his head, shrugged and held his head up proudly, he found he could look at the shining castle without blinking or damaging his eyesight.

The great door of the castle creaked and creaked, swayed, rattled and murmured something.

Sidney and his companions looked intently at the great door. A voice from inside the castle hollered, "Young Prince, you`ve done very well! You have the keys to the King Dom!"

Sidney called boldly at the great door, "Open up! I know all the secrets!"

Some distance away, they heard a grumbling, painful voice, saying, "Oh, terror! Terror! Terror! Does this mean I`m going to be defeated!" Then a whistling wind through cracks and crevices, then silence.

The great door sagged, groaned and coughed! The castle hummed and moved in time with the humming.

Sidney`s body began to glow.

The castle suddenly pulled itself up from its foundations and slowly began to rise in the air.

"Are you going to dance? Have your fun!" Sidney called to the golden castle. "When you`re satisfied, come back to us!"

The castle rose higher and higher in the sky which was bright and hot. Birds, butterflies and flowers circled the castle.

Reavis, Stephanie and William stared with wide open mouths, their eyes radiating beams.

Then slowly, the castle came back down, when it touched its foundations, a voice flew out of the castle, "The King awaits!"

Books began to fall from the sky again like rain all around Sidney and his companions with pages turning quickly.

There was one book which came fluttering over and around Sidney, its pages were empty But on the cover and spine were written: THE MAN WHO LOVED STEPHEN KING.

Sidney was overwhelmed with joy.

A voice spoke from the book: "Write me! Write me! Tell the literary world!"

Sidney was filled with a sense of complete accomplishment.

The door of the golden castle shook!

The sun came down and kissed Sidney`s joyful face and he wasn`t burnt nor blinded and he said, "All hail the King!" and smiled from the depths of his soul.

Rock-and-Roll music was heard some yards away.

The sun shone with every colour of the world.

Sidney took the deepest of breaths, took hold of the cartridge-pen and tapped the great door which swung open wide and a voice from inside called "Hurrah! Hurrah!"

"Everything is possible from the pen of Stephen King!" Sidney and his companions chanted.

"Gnik Nehpets is King`s name spelt backwards!" Sidney called happily.

A purple dargon groaned, rushed out of the castle and flew away howling for mercy then exploded.

Inside and all around outside the glittering golden castle there were fireworks and joyous laughter.

Sidney`s past reading life spun before him like on a movie or television screen. He and his companions came into the castle and into a large hallway and into a room off the hallway, Stephen King was seated in front of a computer on a table on a stage, dressed in a black suit, bow-tie, white shirt and shining black shoes and he was smiling.

Is he about to receive the Nobel Prize? Sidney thought. What strange vision.

A ghost of the poet Robert Browning appeared and remarked, "No, not yet," and disappeared.

Sidney and his companions were excited beyond belief.

"We`re in the hands of Stephen King," Sidney said to his friends.

His companions began to hum sweetly.

"Welcome, sweet Prince!" King wrote on the computer-screen.

Lightning flashed! Thunder burst outside! But King was smiling. "Hold on to the pen!" he said to Sidney.

A tall figure with no face, dressed in crimson, appeared, "Aha! We meet face to face and in some kind of flesh!" it snarled at Sidney and his companions. "What have you got left to free him!"

"There`s no way you can touch me!" Sidney replied.

The tall crimson faceless figure growled, howled, barked, grunted and urinated blood. "All the evil in the books are going to fuck you away!" it bawled.

"Genius is in the pen, friend!" Sidney chimed and help up the cartridge-pen. "We`re going to write you off!" he said to the tall figure.

"Write it as I want it!" the tall crimson figure raged. "Re-write the blasted thing or I`ll end the days of light of your reading world!"

"Not a chance!" Sidney answered.

The tall figure coughed and urinated pus and blood.

"Hold on to the pen tightly!" King wrote on the computer again.

Sidney brought all the pressure in his body on the pen, concentrating deeply.

"Oh, jealous evil, come to my aid!" the tall figure growled and a foul stench was coming it was beginning to enter the nostrils of Sidney and his friends.

"Oh, we aren`t touched by the stench!" Sidney said, smiling.

Reavis, Stephanie and William were also smiling.

Sidney waved the cartridge-pen above his head and a book appeared, flying around, its covers opening and he and his companions were lifted and taken into the large book which now flew around Stephen King`s head, then the book get smaller and smaller and went into King`s wide open mouth and the book was swallowed.

"What! What!" roared the tall figure, changing from crimson to yellow then back to crimson again. "I know you`re still alive! The four of you are hiding in there! But to get at you, I`ll have to remove the invisible barrier holding King! I know you can hear me! Come out! Or I`ll destroy everything, even myself!"

"You`re about to end!" came on the computer-screen and King smiled.

"The sword is mightier than any pen!" the tall figure screamed. "I`m my own literary creation! I`m an inspiration for most fiction in the world! I can`t be done away with! No! No! No!" and the tall figure turned blue and green. "I`m fiction`s nightmare!"

King opened his mouth wide and the book with Sidney and his friends came out and they resumed their normal size, standing erect and proud.

"Aha! Fuck the four of you!" the tall figure fumed. "I want to be free too! I want independence! I don`t want any damn writer to control me!"

Sidney heard a voice which only he could hear, saying, "Leave me alone! I know nothing of my son`s whereabouts!" it was his mother`s voice or sounded like her.

They heard a mobile-phone ringing.

Sidney tapped his head with the cartridge-pen and the voice disappeared.

"We`re the perfect soul-mates!" he called out. "Jealous, misunderstanding critics are destruction! Stephen King bestrides the literary world like a colossus! Make a circle again!"

Sidney and his friends formed a circle around King and walked around slowly chanting his name: "Stephen King! Stephen King! Stephen King!"

The tall figure cringed, farted, urinated, spun around and grovelled.

"King is writing a new novel! Who can guess what it is about?" Sidney jeered at the grovelling tall figure.

King`s face began to change into the faces of dead Nobel Prize winners, all smiling.

"Fuck you, children of whores!" the tall figure blasted.

"Through the eyes of Maine, we see him strong!" Sidney and his companions chanted.

"Clever reader with that clever pen!" the tall figure rolled about, shaking, farting, urinating, stomach growling, "Black is white and white is red! Horror is shit! Blood-suckers come out! demons eat the pages! Fire burn the books! Aliens from outer space come to my aid!"

Sidney and his friends danced and danced around the now wailing tall figure, chanting:

"All the literary agents and publishers in the world are on our side!"

"Hold on tighter!" Sidney said.

The tall figure writhed on the floor.

"United we stand reading forever!" Sidney and his companions called out bravely.

"I`m called by many names and appearances!" the writhing tall figure bawled, "Don`t write me off, King! Don`t kill me off! You couldn`t do it without these brave readers! Oh, the

Horror! Horror! Horror! The literary world is full of horrors!"

Stephen King was smiling at his computer.

"Writers of the world unite!" Sidney called out, "You`ve nothing to lose but rejection-slips!"

"Every witch and demon in hell are in those rejection-slips, boy!" the tall figure screamed.

As Sidney and his companions danced and held onto each other tightly, Stephanie sank and sat on the marble floor which was warm, she lifted and opened her legs wide, Sidney touched her stomach with the cartridge-pen and her stomach swelled, she became pregnant, Sidney kissed the cartridge-pen and indicated that Reavis and William do the same, they both kissed the pen. Sidney touched Stephanie`s stomach with the pen again and she changed and became Stephen King`s wife, Tabitha with a joy on her face as Sidney, Reavis

William called on her to push.

Meanwhile, the tall figure staggered up, drunk-like and now began to turn grey all over, howling for all kinds of mercy, "Don`t send me to perdition!"

"Push! Push! Push!" Sidney, Reavis and William said to King`s wife, Tabitha.

The tall figure now totally grey, stood, stone-like, a statue, began to crack all over.

"Push! Push! Push!" Sidney and his now two companions told Tabitha who was pushing with all her strength.

The tall figure cracked and cracked and crumbled to the marble floor into a heap of grey dust which blew away in a sudden gust of wind from the opened great door.

The cry of a baby was heard coming from between Tabitha`s legs, but instead of a human baby, a thick book came out, its pages empty and turning-crying.

Then Stephen King came to them and taking the new born book, said, "What a story this is going to be. I`ve created all this to show that any fan who might be thinking of kidnapping me, to think again. If they think they are going to knock me over with a van and then hold me captive, it won`t work. My imagination is beyond such things. An ardent fan is a serious reader who truly understands my work like Sidney Prince."

Tabitha rose from the floor, kissed her husband, smiled and said, "I`m going to the bathroom. It`s been a long time coming. This new book is going to be a winner" and she excused herself and left the room. She didn`t seem to be agonized or worried.

"So we are characters in your imagination waiting to be born?" Sidney asked, looking at his companions.

"Yes, you certainly are," King replied matter –of-factly. "As I`ve said, you were created for this quest to ward off greedy ransom-seekers and jealous critics."

Sidney, Reavis and William turned into Dali-like painting images and went into the turning pages of the new-born book King held in front of them.

Rock-and-Roll music was now heard all over the castle which was now disappearing.

The voice of a Little Richard-like singer screamed: "Kidnappers beware! Don`t say you don`t care! We know your every move! You`ll never get in the groove! Wow! Wow! Wow!"

And in every new book by Stephen King, Sidney Prince, the man who loved King, appeared in some form or other.